Born in Stairfoot in South Yorkshire, Raymond Hunt
moved with his family to Dudley when he was seven.
He joined the RAF in 1944 and was posted to India
in 1945. He married his late wife Jean in 1950.

Raymond worked as a mechanical/structural engineering
designer before his retirement at the age of 64, when he
and his wife toured every continent except Antarctica!

Austin Macauley published the first volume
of Raymond's *Heterogeneous Poems* in January
2022 and the second in March 2023.

RAYMOND HUNT

Jenny Taylor's Emoji

AUSTIN MACAULEY PUBLISHERS™
LONDON • CAMBRIDGE • NEW YORK • SHARJAH

A CIP catalogue record for this title is available from the British Library.

ISBN 9781398487192 (Paperback)
ISBN 9781398487208 (ePub e-book)

www.austinmacauley.com

First Published 2024
Austin Macauley Publishers Ltd
1 Canada Square
Canary Wharf
London
E14 5AA

J ENNY TAYLOR WAS a pleasant girl. She wouldn't
say boo to a goose, and she wouldn't hurt a fly; but
unfortunately, she had this Emoji, or you could call it an
affliction, with her left eye, and it got her into all kinds
of trouble you wouldn't believe. On one occasion she was
talking to Rob Smith and Sue his wife, when she winked.
Now Sue was fairly broad-minded and was going to let
it pass, when Jenny did it again. Well, this was just too
much for Sue, and without a word, she just let swing
her handbag at Jenny, but unfortunately, her aim was a
bit too low, and instead of hitting Jenny, all the drinks on
the table went flying off the table across the floor. Broken
glass, beer, the girls' drinks, ashtrays and the like: the pub
landlord was not impressed. He came over and with a few
choice words.

"I'm having no more of this, you will have to leave."

Sue said, "It was her fault," pointing a finger at Jenny,
who turned a deep shade of pink and clenched her teeth,

"You will have to pay for the damage," the landlord said.

Jenny said, "I'm not paying, it was her doing."

Sue said, "You made me do it, winking at my husband."

Jenny said "I did not, I wouldn't touch him with a barge
pole."

Well, this caused another furore, and on it went. Rob
was getting fed up with this lot, and he said, "How much
do I owe you, landlord?"

The landlord said, "Three quid should cover it."

Rob paid up and said, "I'm off. You can sort this lot out
yourselves." So off he went.

Jenny turned to Sue. They had been friends for a long time, but the affliction must have been getting worse, because Sue hadn't noticed it before.

Jenny said, "I would not do that anyway. You know me better than that."

Sue said, "Well, you did it."

Jenny said, "Well, I wasn't aware of it. I must see if I can sort it out."

Sue said, "There, you did it again."

Well, the two girls chatted about it for some time and agreed that it was not worth breaking up a friendship over it.

At this particular period in her life, Jenny was always getting into trouble, but before I tell you about that incident, I must tell you what happened at the Rose and Crown.

This happened many years ago.

In those days, beer used to be delivered in wooden barrels and the deliveries were made on horse-drawn carts, usually by a shire horse. They were big horses, very strong but gentle. On this day, there was due to be a delivery to the Rose and Crown in the High Street. Now, in those days, barrels of beer were put into cellars through the cellar doors in the pavement near the road, for convenience, down a ramp into the cellar.

The delivery had been made as usual, and the drayman had departed, but unfortunately, the landlord had, as usual, allowed the drayman to lock the cellar doors on the pavement before he went away. Well, he didn't do a very good job, there was a problem, they were insecure, so you can guess what happened next.

Bill Shakespeare, a regular at the pub, walked over these cellar doors, now Bill was a good 16 stone, and the doors collapsed, well Bill went down the cellar asome over jasome, and landed on his back, concussed, the landlord heard the commotion and dashed down the cellar, from inside the pub, seeing Bill lying there, shouted, "Get a doctor, quick!"

The doctor arrived, checked Bill over, and found there were no broken bones. Bill started to revive, and the doctor said, "We will have to get him to the hospital."

Bill sniffed, looked around and said, "No, leave me here for an hour or two. I'm sure I'll be alright, but leave me a pint glass, in case I get thirsty."

The landlord said, "He's OK, I'll stay with him for a while."

And so it goes on.

Now this tale about Jenny: same pub, but the old landlord had retired, and a new one had taken over, some six years ago… Anyway, Jenny was sitting at the bar, chatting to everyone or anyone who wished to have a word. Now, Beatey, the landlord's wife, was a no-nonsense person: she carried quite a bit of weight and had a solid punch, so don't mess with Beatey. Because of Jenny's affliction, while she was talking to the landlord, Beatey caught sight of the wink – well, can you imagine? She came over to Jenny and threw a pint glass with slops in it all over Jenny, then came round the bar, picked Jenny up and threw her out of the pub.

"Don't come back," Beatey cried.

Well, poor Jenny, what a problem.

Jenny went home, had a shower, put on some clean clothes, and vowed that the next day she would make an appointment to see the doctor. On the following day, she rang the surgery and made an appointment to see Dr Sylvia Hathaway. Sylvia was dark-haired and fairly attractive, a woman in her mid-fifties of slender build and well dressed, quietly spoken and with an Irish accent. She had a friendly disposition and was a very likeable person. She was intelligent and, though not stern, would expect you to conform to her directives. Jenny had made the appointment for Wednesday at 10.30 am.

Wednesday, of course, was market day, and at that time of day the hustle and bustle of the market were in full swing. Of course, Jenny, without thinking, had made the appointment for this time and on this day, without prior thought of the consequences.

The day arrived, and Jenny got up early. She didn't want to be late for her appointment. She got dressed, after attending to her ablutions. She wanted to look her best, so she had purchased a new skirt at the weekend. Unfortunately it was a little too tight, but she decided it was what she would wear to go to see the doctor. She was early so instead of going by bus, she decided that she would walk. It wasn't far, so off she went. She walked past the market stalls. There were a few wolf-whistles and cat-calls, but she took no heed. But then a fellow came up to her and said, "Did you know that the label is dangling down from the back of your skirt?"

Jenny looked down then up to the man and winked.

"No, NO, I'm a happily married man and have a couple of lovely kids."

Well, Jenny just went red, she was so embarrassed. He rushed off one way and Jenny quickly carried on towards the doctors in the opposite direction, still perspiring profusely from that encounter.

She arrived at the surgery in good time, so she had some time to wait until she was called. She went on winking and blinking until she was called into Dr Sylvia's consulting room. The people in the waiting room didn't pay much attention to Jenny, who was avoiding them and was looking out of the window most of the time, in order that they would not see her contortions, trying to hide her affliction.

As Jenny approached the doctor, Dr Sylvia said to her, "What can I do for you today, Jenny?"

They knew each other fairly well. It was only a small village, and as happens in this kind of small village, everyone knows everyone else. After Jenny explained the last two incidents to the doctor, Dr Sylvia could only sympathise with her dilemma. She tried to console Jenny with a few encouraging words and assured her that she would be able to fix the problem, for which Jenny told her that she was very grateful. The doctor put some drops into Jenny's eye to relax the muscle. She gave her some tablets and a patch to cover her eye.

Well, can you imagine? After leaving the surgery and on the way home, Jenny had to pass the market again, and of course there were calls of "Where's your wooden leg?" and "Hello Long John". She thought it was almost as bad as having the wink. Jenny eventually made her way to the edge of town and cursed herself for not getting the bus.

Jenny was 23 years old and had had a quiet life living on the farm until she was 20. Then she decided that she wanted to have an independent life, living on her own doing her own thing. There were quite a few cottages that belonged to the farm. There was one on the edge of the farm, and not too far from the village. This one had become vacant, and Jenny asked her dad if she could have it, and of course, he said yes. The farm was three miles away from the village but was still a good walk away from the cottage.

She visited the farm quite often. Her father had insisted on it before he let her have the cottage, so although she didn't live there, she spent quite a lot of time there. She had two brothers and a sister. They were all older than

Jenny, and Doris, who at 32 was the eldest, she had quite a tale to tell, which we will come onto later, but the two brothers were quite different in character. The eldest of the two, Tom was a fitness fanatic. He was always pitting his muscular strength against the elements, either lifting or pulling or anything else that he thought might enhance his physical capability. He even tried to lift the back end of a cow, with rather disastrous results: the cow was having none of it and let fly with her two back legs, and poor Tom was despatched, flying through the air and landing on his backside. He was not amused.

Now Fred was a different type. He was a quiet, unassuming sort of character, not easily roused, but he wouldn't stand any nonsense either. Now each of the brothers was over 6 feet tall and they were around 175 pounds in weight, and they were very protective of their little sister Jenny, and she knew it. So, rather than create a fuss, Jenny thought that although she knew the ones who were cat-calling her by the market, she thought it better not to mention it to her brothers, so that there would be no repercussions, because she knew what the boys would do.

Now Doris, being the eldest, was the guiding light for the rest of the children. Although they were in their twenties, they very much took notice of what Doris was saying. She was very sensible and quite intelligent. Jim, the dad, and Gladys, the mum, took charge of the running of the farm, so that's the Taylor family.

Two years earlier, Jim had been approached by the local borough council to buy some of his land. The council had previously been instructed by the government to purchase land for the building of council houses. The government had afforded them a loan for that purpose, so Jim, being the good citizen that he was, had no choice, because if he did not agree, then a compulsory purchase order would be implemented. Knowing this, Jim gladly accepted their offer to compensate him for the loss of both earnings and future livelihood, so that was that. Jim still had quite a few acres of land left, and being the astute man that he was, realised that there were pickings to be made from the council's venture into the building of council houses. Since there were no existing shops in the locality, and since no new ones had yet been built, at that time, he would venture into the grocery business. Besides that, he knew that, in those days, the building of houses required limestone, which would be used for the ceilings in the houses.

So Jim, as I said, was an astute man, so he had built two limestone-cracking kilns, which would crack the chunks of limestone into powder, which could then be used for building. His venture into the groceries business was where Doris came into the picture: she would manage the shop, which of course was part of the farmhouse, and would purchase the goods, which was made easy by representatives of the various organisations, being only too happy to call to implement orders and future orders from Doris.

This all went fairly well. The farm was functioning more or less as normal and everyone seemed happy with the situation, and of course, because the farm had been reduced in size, it meant that they all had a little more free time, except Doris of course. It also meant, now that some of the houses had been built, that she was inundated with people coming for groceries and other household requirements. The farm had 60 chickens now: the stock had been increased because of the local population's need for eggs and chickens. The days of battery hens were just beginning to take shape, but the odd chicken for Sunday dinner was deemed to be a luxury. The farm also housed 24 ducks, and of course, duck eggs were a somewhat scarce commodity. The rabbit population, in the early days, were also a menace to farmers because they used to eat the crops, so culling of rabbits was an essential undertaking. Not only that, but they were also used as an occasional meal. They were hung in the farm shop and bought by the customers and were in great demand.

Jim, of course, went out on his daily round to various long-standing customers, in and around the village, with milk and eggs, and various other things now that the shop was in full swing, for which, he was assured, they were very grateful. Dolly the horse knew the round better than Jim. On one occasion, even, Jim was having a pint in one of the pubs towards the end of his round. Dolly, of course, had her nose bag on, but decided that she had had enough and decided to head off home. No one was more surprised than Jim to find that when he came out of the pub, the horse and cart had gone. He was not amused, so he made his way back to the farm, where everyone was hilarious about the horse leaving Jim behind. Anyway, the horse had been attended to by Tom and was in good shape, no harm done.

Jenny liked dancing, and used to go to the village hall on a Saturday night, as did all the locals, for a bit of a jig and a drink and some refreshments. It was quite an occasion. Tom and Fred were there too, of course. Tom also used to flex his muscles around the girls, who used to have a bit of a giggle at his antics. They all thought it was funny him prancing about like a peacock to gain their attention, and Tom used to love it. Most of the girls thought he was a twit, but some used to like it. Anyway, it didn't deter him from doing what he wanted to do.

Fred, of course, was quite the opposite. He just sat among both boys and girls and talked, making general conversation about local events and what each of them had been doing over the last week – local gossip. One of the girls mentioned that Jenny had been tormented about her affliction. Fred said he would have a word with the perpetrator of this innuendo, but apart from that most of the talk was about local events. The evening went off without any problems.

Tom was not involved in the conversations that would be attributed to the goings on with Jenny, so he didn't have to flex his muscles to show his dominance. Fred took Jenny home. He was not on this occasion involved with any of the local females, which was rather unusual because Fred was a nice chap and most of the local girls liked him. He dropped Jenny off and carried on back to the farm. His motorbike was a transverse Douglas 300cc; he used it quite a lot for both business and pleasure. The girls liked it too.

Doris, as I said, looked after the shop. She had been involved with a young man some years ago, for a couple of years. He was one of the local farmers' sons, whose name was Joe, a nice chap from all accounts. He wanted Doris to marry him, then the two of them would immigrate to New Zealand. He was obsessed with the idea that sheep farming in New Zealand: South Island was his foremost ambition, and he was determined to go out there and do exactly that. But Doris was not impressed with that idea, then apparently he booked his passage on a liner and asked Doris to go with him and she refused, so the liaison finished. But they still write to each other. He married an Australian girl named Sue, and they now have two children: a boy and girl. But his wife doesn't mind; she knows all about his friendship with Doris. In fact, they intend to come back to his parents' farm to stay a while, so I've no doubt that she will meet Doris then. They have a farmhand who helps with the sheep, all 300 of them. The farmhand told them he would look after the farm while they were away. Joe said, "May, June – our winter."

He told Doris that they would wait until their daughter, the younger sibling, was old enough to understand what was going on, so that would be perhaps next year. Doris was looking forward to seeing the family, so with his own family and Doris and her family – they knew each other very well, just living next door – there was going to be quite a party.

Jenny was keen on one of the boys in the village, but he was not keen on having an affair with any of the local girls at the moment. He was preoccupied with an investigation in which he was involved, being a detective sergeant in the Royal Constabulary. He had confided in Jenny, to some extent, to get some information from her about the investigation. He probably went too far in divulging more than he had intended or was allowed. However, that said, he told Jenny the whole story so far, as follows.

Apparently, a fellow was walking in the woods nearby when he saw a shiny object in the brook. He retrieved the object to find that it was a gold watch, and still in good working order. There was also a smouldering campfire nearby and a canopy where someone had been sleeping overnight. There was also a lady's handbag with three letters inside. That information and the contents of the letters were not divulged at this time. Jenny, of course, was quite intrigued that she was singled out to help in the investigation. She frequented the woods often: she was quite interested in ornithology and spent some time making notes of visits by different birds to the locality. However, she had not seen anything unusual that might help in the investigation, as far as she was aware.

Getting back to the intended party that took place when Joe returned… Joe and Sue and the two children came back to stay with Joe's parents for what was intended to be an eight-week stay. Things didn't quite work out that way. Doris and Joe had quite strong feelings for each other, of which both families were aware, and poor Sue, although she knew what had occurred, some years earlier, was resigned to the fact that, although Joe was still fond of her, things were not quite the same as they had been before they left New Zealand. And to top it all, two weeks into the holiday, Joe's dad became seriously ill, and had to go into hospital. He had had a heart condition for some time but had been doing his job. Being a farmer, and running the farm was a full-time job. However, while Joe was here, he had to take over running the farm because of his father's condition. His mother did help out, but there were lots of jobs, mending fences, etc., that she could not do; even his father had to contract some jobs out because of his condition. So Joe had a lot of repair work to do, so it now became a full-time job, which of course exacerbated the problem.

Joe and Sue had a long talk about their future and what they were going to do about the farm in New Zealand and this farm here in the UK. Eventually, they came to the conclusion that the only way out of the problem was that Sue should take the girl back to New Zealand and look after the farm there, with the help of the farmhand left in charge, and Joe and the boy stay here on this farm.

Joe's mother was involved. She was pleased that they had decided that their farm would now be taken over by Joe. She was worried that they would go back to New Zealand and that she would have to employ someone to look after the farm for her. So that was a relief for Joe's mum and dad. Joe's mum was happy that the boy would stay here also, but sorry that Sue would be going back home. the farm was always intended to go to Joe anyway, so that was the way it turned out.

While they had been here, Doris had become a very good friend to Sue, had taken her to the various events that were taking place in the locality, out shopping and to restaurants and bars, and taken her to see the sights: to the zoo, the castle, to all the places of interest, in the area. Although they had their differences, to do with Joe, he was working and Joe's mum was looking after the child, to her delight, and the shop was beginning to wind down, because of the local shops which had been built, so both of them had lots of free time to spare, which gave them a golden opportunity to go out together. Sue had said that she should cut short the visit, but Doris persuaded her to do otherwise and stay for the full eight weeks.

The weeks rolled by, then finally came the time for Sue and her daughter to say goodbye and return back to their home in New Zealand. It was a sad occasion for them all, but Sue had promised to come back again before too long. Doris said that she would go to Sue's farm to spend a few weeks during our winter (their summer), at the end of this year. Sue had said that she would be looking forward to it.

Sue went home and things generally got back to normal. Letters were exchanged between the families from time to time. Joe was pleased to know that Sue was managing to cope with the help of Desmond, the farmhand who was looking after the farm while they were in England, so the only thing that worried Joe Martin was his father, whose condition had improved, but he was still unable to do very much, except to look after his own hygiene, so Joe had to go on looking after the farm. If he needed help for anything urgent, the Taylor boys were always there to give a hand. It was always that way, except in unusual circumstances when outside help was required.

Doris spent quite a lot of time over at the Martins' place, looking after Peter, the little boy, together of course with Joe's mum. She would look after the general running of the house and Joe's dad, so Doris would take Peter on various trips to places of interest in the locality, so she had a companion, which was to her liking. Doris spending so much time at the Martins and seeing Joe there, the old attachments began to flourish once again, and with Sue being on the other side of the world, the longing for that liaison began to fade, and Joe began to go out with Doris, taking Peter with them too.

In the meantime, Jenny decided that she was not going to be left out of this police investigation, so she took it upon herself to do a bit of research, to see if she could find out a little more about what was going on with the watch. Why was it in the brook? How was it that the log fire, when first seen, was still full of burning embers? Who had been sleeping under the canopy? Lots of questions to be answered, so her first objective was to ask around the village to see if any of her friends had seen or heard of any unusual gossip going round the village.

It came out, while Jenny was talking to one of her close friends, that one of the single girls in the village had been seen in the woods with a man. Although the man could not be identified, because they were too far away, she knew who the girl was by her attire and her long blonde hair. (Girls generally are attentive to that kind of thing; they usually know the latest fashions and the trends in the village.)

The girl was the same age as Jenny and when she was told that the girl's name was Maud, she instantly rec-ognised that the girl had been in the same class in high school. Jenny said that that was no real surprise, because the girl apparently was a bit of a flirt, and would go off with any Tom, Dick or Harry. The next thing that Jenny had to do was to try to gain the confidence of Maud to see if she was the one to whom the watch belonged. How to do that without raising suspicion was going to be quite a challenge, but Jenny had to devise a plan to do just that, which she did.

The friend who had been giving her this information, whose name was Sarah, was the one she knew would probably be able to give her the information she was seeking, so when the occasion arose, during a get-together that Jenny had arranged with Sarah, the discussion came up about school days, what went on and so forth. The subject of Maud came up and both said what a flirt she was, then Jenny chipped in that there had been gossip in the village about a couple being seen in the wood, and that Maud was the girl but they didn't know who the fella was.

Sarah couldn't throw any light on that but went on to tell Jenny of an incident which had occurred at the local dentist's practice some weeks earlier. Apparently, Maud had made a visit to the dentist's, and Bob Jones, who was the dentist, had accidentally slipped while carrying out an inspection of Maud's teeth and fallen on top of Maud. He was about to apologise when Maud threw her arms round him and gave him a bear hug. He smiled, disentangled himself and asked his assistant if she could go and get something from the storeroom. His assistant, whose name was Jean, was a 16-year-old, but thought it rather odd that this request should be made. It had never been made before.

Nevertheless, she did what she was told to do. She retrieved the item, which she thought was totally unnecessary, and then came back to the consulting room. When she arrived back she saw that both Bob and Maud were rather red-faced and a little embarrassed. Jean was telling Sarah that something had been going on which made them both look red-faced. Following that incident she, Jean, had become aware that Maud had been making rather an unusual number of visits to the surgery. When Jean made a comment about this to Bob, just being interested, Bob had said that Maud needed an amount of calculus removed from around her teeth; that was the reason for so many visits. Jean accepted that explanation and didn't think any more about it, except that she had been making rather a lot of visits to the stock room, for items that were already available in the consulting room. A search had to be made and, on a few occasions, it took a long time for the items to be found.

Jenny and Sarah were wondering if this liaison was at all connected to the incident in the wood. Jenny had confided in Sarah the information that she herself had been given, in the strictest confidence. Being a bit nosy, this was going to be Jenny's quest. She did know Jean, the dentist's assistant, and made it her next encounter to try to get to see Jean. Then she would ask her to somehow try to find out if Maud had lost a gold watch. This venture worked out rather well, because while Maud was on a visit to the dentist the following week, Jean had asked Maud, "What is the time?" Unknowingly, Maud had said that she had lost her gold watch, and asked Jean if she knew of anyone who may have found it. Of course, Jan said she didn't but would ask around to see if she could find out if anyone had found it, for her. With that Maud thanked her, and then left the consulting room.

Jean contacted Jenny and gave her the information, then asked Jenny if she had the watch. Jenny said no but told Jean not to tell anyone else about this, because the police were looking into the matter. So it seemed that that was another part of the puzzle solved.

Jenny decided not to tell her policeman friend, Roger Carlton Perry. Roger was a bright young man of 29 years of age, a university graduate who had risen in police ranks rather more quickly than would normally be the case. His father was the Chief Inspector of Constabularies, which lots would say was why he advanced in the constabulary ranks so quickly, and much more quickly than normally would be the case. Jenny was to try to meet him again, to try to extract more information from him.

Jenny met Roger at the local Saturday night dance, although this was not the time or place for their discussion. Instead, a meeting was arranged at the gym.

Jenny met Roger at the gym on the following Wednesday. They get on well together, they have similar interests: bird watching, archery, hockey, and various pastimes, and of course the local gym club. Jenny had previously mentioned to Roger that she had some information about the investigation while at the dance last Saturday, so he was rather keen to hear what she had to say. She had said that it was only hearsay and she said that it was what she had heard, which was of course a fib. Roger mentioned that he had made very little progress on the matter, Jenny asked him about the letters. After explaining that someone had lost a gold watch but that they hadn't yet found out who that someone was, he did say that the three letters were in plain envelopes with transparent windows for the names and addresses, but the names and addresses had been deliberately removed so that they were not identifiable.

The name of the sender of one was still there. It was from a local solicitor. One of the others was a love letter, and the other was a bill from the local council. Jenny was only interested in the one from the solicitor and their name. She could then find out, she hoped, if one of her friends, or their friends, knew someone who worked in the solicitor's office, then perhaps she could get the information she was looking for. It turned out that a friend of a friend knew Beth, the solicitor's clerk who worked in that office. It turned out that Jenny knew Beth as an acquaintance – it was a small community, after all. Beth was quite a bit older than Jenny, so although they knew each other, she was not one of Jenny's close friends. Jenny found out that Beth was a keen archery enthusiast, so she made a point of meeting her at one of their sessions. She approached Beth and began by chatting about various things. Then she came to the point where she asked her about her work at the solicitor's office. Jenny told her what she knew and asked if she could throw any light on the subject. Jenny asked her directly if one of those standard letters she had previously referred to had been sent to Maud. Beth said that she would be in deep trouble if she told anyone about the kind of information that had come from their office, but she nodded her head, although not saying a word. Jenny thought the answer was in the affirmative. She thanked Beth and told her that any information she had given would only be divulged to the constabulary.

Jenny knew that another part of the puzzle had been solved. Jenny spent quite a bit of time deliberating what she could do next, to try to solve why the watch was in the brook, why the fire had still been burning, and if Maud had been the one sleeping under the canopy. That factor could be a possibility. She decided that the next step was to approach Maud and try to gain her confidence. The ace card, of course, was that the constabulary were involved. If Maud knew this, it could help to get to the crux of the matter, so Jenny decided that was how it would be. Of course, Maud could tell her to mind her own business.

However, the constabulary investigation might help in this regard.

Jenny had gathered quite a lot more information about the goings-on in the wood. She had pieced together the facts prior to the occasion in the woods with Maud and Bob Jones, the dentist. And there was his wife's involvement: the solicitor's letter sent to Maud, saying that if she didn't keep away from her husband, she would be faced with serious consequences. Maud had taken heed of this threat. She told Bob that she no longer wished to carry on this association and mentioned the threat that had been made against her. But he dismissed it and said that she was bluffing. However, Maud was adamant and told him it was finished. Bob then said if she didn't carry on as before, he would come after her. She took that to be a threat!

That is where the occasion of the woods came into it. Bob Jones had been harassing Maud to the point where she was afraid to leave her flat and he was trying to force his way into her flat through a closed, locked door. She thought the only way to avoid him and escape from his clutches, was to find a place in the woods where she could hide. She hoped that he wouldn't find her and that it would all blow over and his wife would threaten to divorce him. All sorts of things went through Maud's mind in the hope that this nightmare would come to an end.

One of the villagers had informed the police of the finding in the wood, but had left everythin as it was, except the watch, which he thought might be swept along with the water. That was handed to the police. Roger Carlton Perry was then put on the case to find out what had happened, and that's when Jenny Taylor became involved. The detective sergeant had told Jenny of this, as you know, but she wondered: was now the time to divulge what she knew? She decided it was the time. She contacted Roger and they agreed, as they did before at the archery venue, that she would reveal all.

Jenny gave him the saga of what she knew and how she had obtained the information. Roger was very impressed and told her so. Jenny suggested that, so as not to alarm Maud, she would arrange with Maud that they, Jenny and Roger, would go to Maud's flat and there discuss the situation with Maud. Roger agreed. Jenny knew that Bob Jones would be at the dental practice when she met Maud. The meeting was arranged, so Jenny passed the information on to Roger.

Maud was very gratified that at last she would get out of the hole she had put herself in. Jenny and Roger met at the allotted time and went along to Mauds flat. She saw them coming and opened the door. Maud said, "Thank you so very much, you can't believe how grateful I am." Then she started crying.

Jenny put her arm round Maud's shoulder and said, "Come on now, it will soon be all over, the policeman will sort it out for you."

Roger said, "Yes, tell me what went on and I'll soon sort it out."

Maud said, "The best way to tell you what happened is for us to go to the wood, and I can show you exactly what took place there."

So off they went. They found the spot with the canopy still in place. The handbag and the letters had previously been removed by the police. Maud said, "Bob Jones had found out where I had been hiding, had followed me and then grabbed hold of me. He started to slap me around. I struggled and got free, then I ran. That was when I must have lost my watch."

The policeman said "We could charge him with aggravated assault."

Maud asked Roger not to prefer charges against Bob but to warn him to stay away from her, otherwise a court order would be placed.

The policeman said, "Leave it with me, and I can assure you that you will have no more trouble from Bob Jones." At that, Roger said, "I will go to the practice right away and sort it out," and off he went.

Maud and Jenny had a cup of tea and a chat. Maud thanked Jenny for helping her. She was so relieved.

While all this was going on with Jenny, things on the farm were still carrying on as usual, except that Tom had had a word with Jim his dad, that he thought he might join the forces and try to get in as a physical training trainee. His thought, he said, was that he would become a physical training instructor if he was dedicated enough to it, that was something he had always been keen on. He had always been popular at the gym for his prowess and his eagerness to advance into doing better at whatever the instructors had commissioned him to do. Pop told him it was his choice to do, if that was what he wanted. Nothing more was said on the subject at that time.

When Tom mentioned it to Fred and asked him if he thought they could cope without him. Fred said they could, and he should carry on and do whatever he wished. Fred said that he was quite content with what he was doing. Since their father was getting on in years and did less on the farm, Fred had taken on more of the work and responsibilities that his dad could not now do, but he was quite happy doing it.

Tom had never been very keen on farming and was determined to seek a different path. The next thing the family knew was that Tom had signed up to join the RAF for a three-year period and said that if things went according to plan, he would probably sign up for a further period. He had been instructed to go to Cosford on a training course – his travel vouchers and instructions had been delivered by post – so 10 days later, Tom said farewell to the family and was on his way.

Meanwhile, Doris had made all the preparations to take the little boy Peter with her to Dunedin, where Joe's and Sue's farm was located, in South Island New Zealand. She had asked her mum if she could cope with the shop and farmhouse. Her mum said she could and that if she needed any help, Pop was there to give a hand, so she had no worries on that score. The farm shop's trade had been running down somewhat, so looking after it was now less of a problem. The volume of trade in the newly built shops was increasing because the variety of products available was increasing, and the number of new houses being built and therefore the number of customers shopping meant that their profit margins were getting better. It all added up to a fall in trade at the farm shop, but there was still enough for it to continue; things like fresh eggs, chicken, ducks, rabbits and much more besides.

Because of the influx of people now living on the council estate, the local Council needed to build a new primary school. The plans had already been drawn up and approved, because it was obvious that one would be needed: the nearest primary school to the estate was over a mile away. The school would comprise of eight class-rooms, a large cloakroom and an assembly hall. In the main building, there would be a playing area, a football pitch, and recreation facilities. The whole project had to be carried out very quickly, and so it was, with enormous success.

Teachers were assembled and the functioning of the school was soon implemented. There was a shortage of teachers for the beginners and first year children, so volunteers were invited to fill the post. Jenny applied and was accepted, but she had to do a crash course, and was duly elected to the post.

Samantha Davidson was the teacher of the 10-year-olds, who would go on then to senior high school. Samantha was 25 years old. She was originally from the south of England but had moved north because houses were a lot cheaper, and she was keen to maintain her independence since leaving home to go to university, so she bought a house in the area.

She frequented the village dance hall on Saturday nights and that is where she met Fred Taylor. Fred took a liking to Samantha and saw her quite frequently. Things started to get more serious when Fred invited Samantha to come to the farm. As it happened, Samantha had been brought up on a farm: her parents were farmers of arable crops in Kent, so there were lots of things that were quite similar and familiar.

They did come. Fred bought her to the farm and they spent some time together with Fred's mum and pop. Samantha eventually became a regular visitor to the farm, and occasionally came for Sunday lunch. Fred's mum Gladys and pop Jim took a liking to Samantha and treated her as one of their own. Then came the day, some time later, when Fred and Samantha decided to become engaged to be married. The Davidsons were invited to stay at the farm and their son Jason was invited to stay with Joe and Doris, if he so wished. He was still at University taking a degree in agriculture, and Joe said, "We could have a talk about sheep farming," which was quite different to what he had been used to. Joe had been at the University of Aberystwyth in Wales and while there had attained an Honours Degree in Agriculture and Engineering. He had also majored in the Welsh language. Although he had the language, he rarely used it, except when prompted by people when visiting parts of Wales where the language is preferred, rather than English, although occasionally the family would attend livestock sales in Wales, mainly to use his expertise in the selection and purchase of animals at auction. It was an attribute that would become useful in later life.

So the time for the planned trip, which Doris had arranged to go to Dunedin, came. Joe kissed and hugged his son, and said, "Say hello to your mum for me."

Three weeks later, they arrived in Dunedin. It was a comparatively easy sea crossing, calling at one or two dropping-off points on the way, but arriving unscathed at the dockside in Dunedin. The meeting at the dockside was all hugs and kisses. The little boy Peter looked anxiously round and at the sight of his mum he started to cry. She rushed forward and held him in her arms to console the poor boy. He had missed his mum so much since she left the UK to go home. The meeting was so sorrowful for them all, but she soon consoled him and told him she had got a lovely present for him when they got home to the farm. Sue introduced Doris to Desmond, and the party then went on to the farm.

When they arrived at the farm you could see that Peter was now in his element. He was running round in every room and in every nook and cranny. It was obvious, his familiarity with the place. It was lovely to see him like that. Sue then took Peter down to the stables, and he was shown the pony she had bought for him. He was thrilled to bits with it. He threw his arms round the pony's neck and then said, "Thank you Mum." He was once again the happy little boy he had always beem.

Later on, when Sue had shown Doris round the place, they got into huddle while Desmond looked after the kids.

They had a lot to talk about, what had been going on, etc. But before that happened, the little girl Jill must have thought that she was being neglected somewhat, and left Desmond and came and snuggled against her mum, who then gave her a little love, and she danced away merrily and went back to Desmond. Sue then went on to tell Doris that Desmond had sold his home and moved into the farm to live, which he had also been doing while they were away in the UK. It was more convenient to look after the farmhouse and the sheep.

Sue said that she had become rather fond of Desmond and thought the feeling was mutual. She had conveyed this to Joe by telegram. Doris said he hadn't mentioned it to her. In the message, Sue said that because of the circumstances, perhaps it would be better if they split up and had a divorce. Doris told Sue that her and Joe had been going out together and taking Peter with them. Both girls were fairly broad-minded, and because the situation was as it was, with Joe having to look after the farm in the UK and Sue looking after the farm in New Zealand, it seemed the best solution all round. There was no animosity between the two girls and both agreed they should contact Joe and get his reaction to what the girls had been discussing. The next few days were spent with that in mind.

Sue had told Doris that she had spoken to Desmond about selling Joe's half of the farm, and he had said that now that he had sold his house he could afford to buy Joe's half. Sue had told Joe of this offer and he had accepted it, conditionally upon the legal outcome.

Little Peter was the next worry. Doris said that the boy was heartbroken not to be with his mum: being away from his mum was a big wrench for him, so something had to be done about it. The most important thing was the happiness of the child. Doris said that although she had purchased his return passage, she thought that the child would be happier if he stayed with his mum. She said he could visit his dad when he was older. When he was told that he could stay with his mum and could visit his dad when he was older or if, as Doris had told Sue, they should all come and visit again, his little face beamed with joy.

On the following day of the visit, Sue asked Doris if she would like to go for a ride round the farm. Of course, being the horse woman that she was, Doris said that she would love to, so they donned suitable riding attire for horse riding and went down to the stables. Sue had four horses, which were used when the sheep were grazing at the far reaches of the farm. She also had two collie sheep-dogs, who had been well trained by Desmond. She decided that they needed a little exercise, so would take them with them. They saddled up and adjusted the stirrups for Doris, then were on their way.

Sue said they would use the bridle path, which went all round the periphery of the farm. Sue told Desmond, who was looking after the children, that they would keep an eye on the sheep on their way round. Desmond would go out later and make a closer inspection and make sure that everything was alright.

Sue and Doris were enjoying the view, the snow-capped mountains in the far distance and the beautiful views all round, when Doris commented that it was spectacular and so wonderful. But looking toward the sheep, she noticed that one of them was limping. She pointed this out to Sue, and Sue said she would have to dismount and deal with it. Doris took her reins and Sue sent the dogs in to separate the lame one from the rest of the flock. She said she would put it into a holding pen and Desmond would bring a tractor-drawn trailer and take the lamb back to the farm. There were several pens located round the farm for such an eventuality occurring. That was quickly executed, to Doris's amazement, and Sue was back on her horse and ready to go.

Doris said, "That was quick."

Sue said, "You have to be when there are so many sheep to look after."

Sue was telling Doris how many newly born lambs that had had to be delivered during the lambing season, and the number was staggering.

Doris continued with her three-week visit and while there helped out in the farmhouse, cooking and looking after the children, while Sue and Desmond could attend to the sheep and do some of the repair work that needed doing in and around the sheds and stables. Desmond had to go out to the sheep, as was his daily routine, to make sure they were okay, the lambing season being over, just to be sure the baby lambs were being looked after by their mothers, and not being abandoned, which does happen. Sue thanked Doris for what she was doing, and said that it had given them a chance to catch up with some of the things that needed to be done. Sue and Doris were able to go out on the town, see some of the historic sites and generally have a tourist's view of the place, the library, town hall, etc. Of course, in the evenings they went to the theatre and the cinema and so on.

Then, of course, the final day of Doris's visit arrived. They all went to the dockside to see Doris depart on her journey back to the UK. It was a heart-rending experience. They were all sad to see her go, particularly Peter, who had grown fond of Doris. They had spent so much time together, particularly during his stay in the UK. She boarded the ferry boat to take her to the International Dock departure bay, where she would get on the liner to the UK, having kissed and hugged them all to say goodbye. They all continued to wave as the boat disappeared from view.

The voyage home was uneventful, calling in at Bombay, then across the Red Sea into the Suez Canal, through the Mediterranean up around Gibraltar then on to Southampton, arriving three weeks to the day she left.

Gladys and Jim were there to greet her, along with Joe. A big smile from them all as she got off the boat, Joe taking on her luggage trolly, hugs and kisses all round. They then proceeded to the railway station where they would catch a train home. They all wanted to know about the trip: were they all alright, what was it like? From Mum and Pop, lots of questions as they boarded the train. Having heard a little from Joe, Doris wished to hear more. It was soon to come, because they had an hour or two to settle down and listen to Doris. Of course, Joe knew all about it, but was a good listener. There were a few private things that Doris had to say to Joe, but there was time for that to come later.

Joe and Sue went through divorce proceedings after Doris had come back from her visit to Dunedin without Peter. She had documents for him to sign: they had decided that this was the best way to keep the documents safe. Sue had explained to Doris what the solicitor had told her before she left, so that there would be no misunderstanding. The sale of Joe's half of the farm, which was bought by Desmond, went through without a hitch.

Doris said, "I have invited Sue, Desmond and the children to visit us, if and when it's convenient. I take it that's OK with you?"

"Of course" Joe said.

They would have to find someone who was trustworthy, to look after the farm while they were away, with a good knowledge of sheep farming, and who could also stay at the farmhouse while doing so. They had quite a number of people in mind who they thought would be good candidates for the job, but it seemed that these people were already employed by farmers in the locality, and they had to be persuaded to co-operate. They were a friendly, co-operative bunch, who from time to time helped each other out, when the need arose. Desmond didn't think that would be a problem; he had worked for sheep and cattle farmers in the past.

Now that Sue and Joe were divorced, Doris and Joe could marry, if they so wished – something that could have happened years ago, before Joe went to New Zealand. It seemed a coincidence but inevitable that they should marry, and that is what they did. Unfortunately, Joe's father died. He eventually succumbed to the heart condition that had troubled him for years, although it was only in the last few years that he had problems carrying out the work he had to do on the farm. It was a very sad time: the two families grieved at their loss.

Joe's mother was a frail lady now. Doris looked after things, but they had to employ someone with nursing experience to come in a few hours a day and help where necessary.

Tom went to Cosford on the allotted day and was assigned to a barrack room with an NCO in charge. He had to take another medical examination, then, after one week at Cosford, he was transferred to a drill and training squadron for his initial induction into the RAF. The course entailed square-bashing drill, armaments training and other extraneous duties, all of which lasted for eight weeks. He was then posted back to Cosford to continue his physical training instructors course.

During his first few weeks at Cosford he met a young lady, also on the same course. She was a blonde, very pretty girl, 6 feet 2 inches tall with blue eyes and of slender build, and with a Yorkshire accent. She came from Horton in Ribblesdale in the Dales. She was a country lass with quite good physical stamina for a woman. She was quiet, gentle and kind and thought she would be a good basketball and hockey player, which as Tom soon found out, was exactly what she did during her university days.

Tom and Fiona – the girl's name – soon became embroiled in a relationship. In the gym, they were both fun-loving people: it was hilarious, some of the things they used to get up to. The other members of the squad laughed and joked with them; they were both very popular. On one occasion Tom tried to do a backflip, but it went horribly wrong, and he ended up face down on the mat. The instructor was not amused, but the others were all laughing. The instructor told Tom not to try anything without his knowledge or approval; he was there to look after their welfare, any bodily harm would be put down to his negligence, his senior officer would put that down on his records, and it would be counted against him in the future. So Tom apologised and said, "Sorry, Sergeant, it won't happen again." They left it at that.

Fiona Brown said, "Tom, you shouldn't do things like that. You could hurt yourself."

Well, the partnership was getting to the stage where Tom was beginning to take notice of what Fiona was saying. It was rather unusual for Tom, because he normally would just hear what they had to say, but then dismiss what he had been told, and continue with whatever he had had in mind. Perhaps the training had had some influence on his behaviour, or perhaps it was Fiona's influence, and he wanted to please her. Whatever it was, things seemed to have changed for him in the past short while – for the better, I might add.

Tom asked Fiona if she would go with him to the farm for the weekend. They both had a bit of leave time to come, and she agreed. The weekend arrived, so dressed in their best uniforms, they set off to visit Tom's parents. They caught the train and arrived, but still had a four-mile trek to get to the farm from the railway station.

Tom began to tell Fiona all about the area, the fossils that he and Fred had found in the underground caves nearby, and that this particular range of hills was at the southernmost end of the Pennine Range, that it was mainly limestone, the fossils were sea creatures deposited millions of years ago. They arrived at the farm. Tom introduced Fiona to Mum and Pop. Tom was as happy as a sandboy, face beaming. They told Fiona to make herself at home, and she was the type of person who would do just that. They all got on very well together. They went on to talk until the early hours of the morning after Fiona had been shown to her room: there were lots to talk about.

Fred had arrived from his evening out. He was introduced to Fiona, had a few words and then said, "If you'll excuse me, I'm ready for bed. See you in the morning," and off he went.

The rest of them continued their conversation for a while, then all agreed it was time to retire.

Mum and Pop were the first down in the morning, and began cooking the breakfast. Fiona was next. She said, "What a lovely smell! I had to get up, I couldn't resist seeing what you were cooking, the smell made me feel hungry. It looks delicious," as she looked down at the breakfast that Mum was cooking.

Tom and Fred were soon roused, and Tom of course wanted to get downstairs to see his Fiona, with a little hug as they met.

"Come on boys." Mum knew that they enjoyed a piled-up breakfast meal to start the day.

"Did you sleep well, Fiona?"

"Like a log," Fiona retorted.

Tom then asked Fiona if she would like to go for a walk round the farm. She said she would, so after breakfast, they set off on their little foray round the farm and up towards the woods on the hill. Meanwhile, back at the farm, the discussion was how they all liked Fiona and how nice she was, and what a surprise it was that Tom hadn't even mentioned Fiona in his letters home, and how calm and considerate that he had become, and of course it was put down to his attachment to Fiona, and his training in the RAF, all to be admired.

Doris and Joe were now married and living at Joe's mum's farm. His father had died. A message had been sent to Doris to tell her that Tom had brought his girlfriend home to the farm, and that they should all come along to Sunday dinner to meet her. Tom and Fiona had to be back at Cosford before midnight on Sunday, so they had to leave late afternoon to walk to the station to catch the train. During the day, Fiona spent most of the time with Tom doing little jobs that needed to be done, and Fred was directing operations, now that he had most of the work to do. Their Pop did very little now, so it was Fred's problem.

The evening arrived, and as usual they would all go to the Saturday night dance at the village hall. It was, as always, a meeting place for families and friends. The local girls, some of them now married, saw Tom in a rather subdued, statesman-like posture, no prancing about and strutting like a peacock anymore, a gentlemanly manner. He nodded to the girls he used to flex his muscles in front of, a different character altogether. His military training had obviously made its mark. Of course, there was Fiona, the girl he intended to marry. It was more important that he was the gentleman that his parents had brought him up to be, when in her company.

Tom had been telling Fred and Samantha that both he and Fiona had agreed that they would continue a lifelong commitment to the RAF and would go on during their working life to retirement from the service. It was their ambition to go to OCTU (Officer Cadet Training Unit) to obtain a Royal Commission as soon as it was practicably possible. Fred and Samantha wished them well and hoped they would achieve their goal.

The evening went off without a hitch. The only late-comer was Jenny. Tom said, "Is everything OK? We have all been wondering if anything was wrong."

Jenny said, "No, everything is OK except that Carlton" – that's what Jenny calls him, his name is Roger Carlton – "had to attend a fracas in a nearby village, which made him late to meet me."

"Oh, that's OK, then," said Tom.

Jenny and Roger (Carlton) were then introduced to Fiona, and the next hour was spent chatting and enjoying each other's company. The evening activity ended and each went their separate ways. Roger took Jenny home, Fred took Samantha home and Tom and Fiona went back to the farm.

The farm shop was open on Sunday mornings, although all the other local shops were closed, and Fiona said to Mum, "Can I come and give you a hand?"

The locals knew the shop was open on Sunday morning, so for any items they may have forgotten could be purchased from the farm, so they were usually busy. Fiona had had some experience as a shop assistant, making a few pounds, while at university, during the vacation.

"Yes, please," Mum said, so their friendship blossomed during that short period.

Tom was in his old working togs and was going to help Fred move some large metal feeding troughs, which he couldn't lift on his own. Gladys, their mum, had given everybody their breakfast and was preparing food for lunch. Jenny had come over early and was chatting to Fiona while they were helping Mum with the food preparation. Fiona was telling Jenny that her father was a blacksmith and farrier in and around the area of Horton in Ribblesdale, in the Dales, Yorkshire. He had a thriving business and employed another farrier to help him.

The farm shop only opened until 12 noon. The morning passed along fairly quickly, they being busy serving customers, then after a cup of tea and a short rest, it was time to start cooking the lunch, it was a special occasion so a little extra was to be prepared, since Tom had brought his bride to be (he said) to the farm where he spent his childhood and to meet the family. The main meal consisted of a nice big piece of pork (lots of crackling), two chickens, and the usual array of vegetables, etc. There would be 10 people at the table.

Mum, Pop, Jo's mum was being brought over, Jo and Doris, Tom and Fiona, Fred and Samantha, and Jenny. Carlton wasn't able to attend because he was on duty, but he had been invited.

The long table had been arranged and all the utensils put in place. Mum would arrange the seating so that no couples would be together or opposite. The moment came: the seats were occupied, Doris and Mum brought in the food and then Pop asked for a moment's silence, so that he could say grace, just a short thanksgiving, then they all passed round their plates to Pop to do the carving.

They all tucked into the food with gusto: it was delicious, they all agreed.

The conversation had been babbling away during lunch, and then on after the sweet had been provided. It went on until it was time for Tom and Fiona to leave. They all kissed and hugged and said goodbye. Tom told his Mum that it would not be too long before he and Fiona came to visit again. She had told Tom that she had thoroughly enjoyed the visit, and wanted to come again soon, and whatever Fiona wants, Fiona gets, according to Tom.

After they had been back at Cosford for nine months, they decided to apply for a commission, they had an interview with an Air Commander and a WRAF Flight Lieutenant, who was taking notes. They, of course, were interviewed separately. They had managed to get the interviews on the same day, so things had worked out well so far.

It was six weeks later when they had a communication that they had to attend another brief hearing – that was how the notice on the noticeboard described it – so they both went along as instructed. They had their interviews independently. Tom went in first. He came away, face beaming. He told Fiona that he had to attend OCTU and was given a date and time. Fiona was a little apprehensive but her time came. Tom told her that things would be OK. She had the interview and also came out smiling. She said to Tom, "Thank God for that. I have to go to OCTU on the same day and time as you," so off they went back to Cosford, smiling and laughing all the way.

While they were doing their training, they thought that perhaps they may be posted to different airfields, and that would be something that neither of them wanted, so they thought the best thing for them to do was to see if they could get married while they were here. They would have liked to have had the wedding at home, but for expediency it would be better to marry while on the base.

So they went to see the Commanding Officer, a Wing Commander Austin. He said, "Why not go and see the Station Chaplain? He will arrange the ceremony for you. We will have to provide living quarters for you when you are married, so next go and see the Admin Officer, tell him I sent you, and he will arrange that for you. It is a little unusual but not unprecedented. I wish you good luck and all the best for the future."

Tom continued the story. "At that, we came away and went to see the Chaplain. The thing to do now was to inform those at home of our decision. We were told that they could all attend the ceremony, but had to leave the base by 6 pm.

'We saw the Admin Officer, Squadron Leader Richards. When we told him what the Commanding Officer had said, he invited us to go along to the accommodation which would be provided. It was very basic, but since the Officers Mess would provide all the food, it was only a few drawers and toilet facilities that were required."

The wedding ceremony took place in the Station Chapel at 11 am. In attendance were Joe and Doris, Fred and Samantha and Jenny. Carlton couldn't make it because he was on duty. Fiona's mum and dad came from the Dales, but Tom's mum and Dad couldn't make it: they had to take care of the farm, but they conveyed their best wishes. Tom said, "Tell them we will come to see them as soon as the opportunity arises."

The Taylor and the Brown families met for the first time. Fiona Brown made the introductions. Fiona had written to them to tell them about the Taylors, so the names were familiar. They soon had familiar topics of conversation to talk about, so that went down well.

The Chaplain went through the proceedings without a hitch. When they left the chapel there was a guard of honour by the door, providing an arch with their rifles. Then it was on to the trainees' mess, with the relatives close behind. The afternoon was a great success, then just before 6pm the visitors all said goodbye and departed for their respective homes. The couple went to their new accommodation. The passing-out parade took place four weeks later, and the couple were posted to RAF High Ercall, near Telford. They had their commissions as pilot officers, and a few weeks later were assigned to help with organising the International Championships at Telford Arena, together with the organising body at Telford Athletic Club.

They visited Tom's Mum and Dad on several occasions after that, together with visits to Fiona's Mum and Pop, over the next year, then they were posted to Cyprus. Many years later, Fiona and Tom had several promotions during their time in the RAF. Finally, Fiona Taylor was assigned to commanding RAF Coltishall as a Wing Commander and Tom as her Adjutant as Squadron Leader Tom Taylor.

After Jenny's escapade with the woods affair and with Maud, she and Carlton became good friends and started going out together. The Perry family were well known to the Taylors, and both families had been to functions and fetes as families and had met and enjoyed their friendship for many years. Roger (Carlton) and Jenny visited the city on occasion to go to concerts modern and classical; they had a wide range of different interests that they both seemed to enjoy together. Roger would be invited to Sunday lunch with the Taylors and Jenny would go to the Perries. Although Jenny had her own farm home, she made it a point that Roger would not be invited there. She said, "Until the day that I get married, that property is sacrosanct, with the exception of family, of course," and that is the way it was before she would even contemplate such a move.

Jenny saw Samantha at school every weekday and noticed, in conversations with Samantha, that marriage seemed to be on her mind quite a lot. Jenny used to see Samantha when she visited the farm usually on Sundays, which is when Jenny would be there, to have Sunday lunch with the family, so she thought she would be nosy and ask Samantha when she and Fred were thinking of getting married. To her great surprise, Samantha said, "We were thinking that perhaps May would be a good time," and that was in less than three months' time.

Jenny said, "Have you told the folks of this?"

"No," Samantha said. "You're the first to know, but now you know, we will inform everyone of our intentions."

Fred was a little shocked that Samantha had let the cat out of the bag, but he was pragmatic about it and told Jenny that it better happen sooner than later.

The families were overjoyed with the news, and now all the preparations had to be got ready for this auspicious occasion: a white wedding. They were all looking forward to it with wild anticipation. The Davidsons, Samantha's family, wanted her to have the wedding at their farm, but she said that this was where she lived, so the wedding would take place here. Samantha and Fred, now that the Taylor family knew of the forthcoming wedding, were to send a message to the Davidson family immediately. Although everyone in the families knew that the event was imminent, they were a little surprised that a leak of some sort had not happened before now. Together, Samantha and Fred, with help from one or two of the Taylors, set about arranging for the forthcoming event. The arrangements were to be made, that on the 22nd of May at 3pm, the marriage of Fred and Samantha would take place in the village church, that the reception after the wedding would be at the village hall, and that their families and a few friends and local dignitaries would be invited to a specially arranged meal, provided by a local establishment.

The next move by the couple was to have the necessary invitation cards printed, as follows, in silver letters with a frilly outer rim to the card and the words,

"Wedding Invitation
To the Wedding of Samantha Davidson,
of Sunny Brook Farm, Kent,
To Frederick Taylor of Old Oak Farm, Worcestershire.
On 22nd day of March at 3pm."

Then the next move was to make a list of all the people they wanted to attend: the families, Mum and Pop Taylor, Mum and Pop Davidson, Doris and Joe, Tom and Fiona – they were away in Australia on a course, so would not be able to attend – Jason Davidson, Jenny and Carlton, Fiona's mum and dad, the Perries (Carlton's mum and dad), the local Mayor, and Jim Taylor wanted one or two more local councillors to come. Doris and Joe asked if it would be OK to invite Sue and Desmond and the children also. "Of course it would," they said.

Joe's Mum would not be able to come: she was in a residential care home, was very frail, and would not be able to attend. That seemed to be all for the moment, but if they had forgotten anybody these could be added later.

The talk between Samantha and Fred was where would they live.

Fred said, "It would be more convenient for me if we lived at the farm, then I could attend to anything that might occur immediately."

Samantha was sympathetic to that need, and said, "We could do that. Then I will have to sell my house and move the furniture to the farm, so that would be OK, but we must go on honeymoon and then stay at my house for the first two weeks after we come back."

So that was agreed. The school was no further away, so it was not a problem.

They then arranged, with Jenny's help, to get a local taxi company to provide a Rolls Royce to take Samantha from her home to the church. Jenny would arrange for the page boys and girls to be at Samantha's house on the day of the wedding. She, of course, would be attending as the Maid of Honour: that pleased Fred and Samantha.

The daylight hours were getting longer and the nights shorter. April Fool's Day had come and gone, everything seemed to be working to plan, so far. Desmond and Sue had arrived from New Zealand with the two children. Peter was now a fine young boy, in his very early teens, and the little girl Jill was growing up to be a beautiful young lady, with quite a lot to say for herself. They were met at the airport by Doris and Joe. When the children saw their dad, they ran to him and loved him. He picked up the little girl and hugged and kissed her and cuddled Peter to his side. The tears ran down his face, he was so happy to see them. He had met Desmond back at the farm; Joe hugged him and Sue, and then Doris hugged and kissed each one in turn. They then left the arrival lounge, chatting away to their hearts' content, got into the car and were on their way to Joe's Farm.

After a brief break, Doris took them over to her mum's farmhouse. They hadn't met Desmond before, so Doris introduced him to the rest of the family, and when it came to Fred and Samantha, Desmond said to Fred, "You don't know what you're letting yourself in for," jokingly, but Fred said, "I think I have a pretty good idea."

Mum and Doris, in the meantime, were preparing a cup of tea and some cake. The conversation then went on to other things, mainly about farming. Peter knew the place inside out, and was showing his sister round, in every nook and cranny, so they too were quite happy.

Jenny had been busy meeting the owners of the Village Hall, which was a private enterprise, to arrange the hiring of the hall with them, on the 22nd of May for the reception and banquet after the wedding of Fred and Samantha. The owners knew them both very well. Jenny went through what was required, tables and chairs, etc. The caterers would be providing tablecloths and serviettes and dining utensils, etc., as well as the meal, which had yet to be decided by Fred and Samantha.

Jenny's next move was to find out what was required for the meal, so she met Fred and Samantha, and they wrote out a list and in what order the meal would be presented, Jenny then approached the caterers, gave them the list and asked them if they could carry out these require-ments on the 22nd of May at 3 pm, and they agreed they could. Jenny informed all the guests that would attend of the arrangements, so that they could make any prepara-tions they needed to make to attend. That done, Jenny approached Fred and Samantha if there was anything more that she could do to help. They thanked her and said if they needed help, she would be the first one they would contact.

Jenny's next move was to get in touch with Carlton to make sure that he could arrange to be available on the day of the Wedding on the 22nd. Jenny went down to the police station to see if she could see Carlton. This was on the Tuesday prior to the wedding, after school, and as she approached the police station, none other than Carlton was getting out of the back of a police van handcuffed to a villain. This man had a slight tan and a black beard. He looked furious: he was obviously not a happy man, but he had no choice but to comply because there were two other policemen in attendance if needed.

This was obviously not the time to approach Carlton. However, she did go into the police station after a short while and left a message for him with the policeman behind the desk, to contact Jenny as soon as possible. They all knew Jenny and her attachment with Roger – not like Jenny and her Carlton; they called him Roger. So that done, she departed back to her cottage.

Waiting for her as she arrived were Doris, Sue and Desmond with the children. Doris knew that Jenny was familiar with the caves and asked her if she would accompany them to go and have a look. The children were very keen, and although Sue had been up there before, she knew that Desmond hadn't, and she liked them, so she would enjoy a return trip.

Jenny said, "Why not? It's been a while since I was up there, so let's go," and off they went.

There were seven arches all joined together, six of them had floors with a large aperture in each, going vertically down. To get underneath those large apertures you had to go down the seventh one, then go underneath the other six: quite a sight. Desmond wanted to go down, but Jenny persuaded him that another time would be better. But he liked what he saw, and said "I will go down, one day."

The others had a good laugh at his enthusiasm. They had a good look. The kids loved it, then returned with Jenny to her cottage and a cup of tea.

When Carlton had finished his tour of duty for the day, having received the message from the desk clerk, he decided, since it was urgent, that he had better go to Jenny's cottage right away. As he arrived, Jenny saw him approach and opened the door.

"What's wrong?" he said. "Why the urgency?"

Jenny said, "I don't know if you realise that Fred's wedding is on Sunday this weekend?"

"Yes, I did know, my Mum told me this morning."

"Have you arranged to have the day off work?" Jenny asked.

Carlton said, "Yes, of course. I don't know why you're bothering your pretty little head over things like this, I did so right away. The Chief Superintendent will also be there." Jenny intimated that Jim her dad must have asked him to attend.

"Well that's OK, then. Now my mind's at rest, less things to worry about." Jenny was poking her nose into everybody's business as usual.

Fred and Samantha had now to arrange their honeymoon. After a long debate and discussion with other members of the family, it was decided that, while they were away, Joe and Doris and Desmond and Sue would look after the farm for them. Although Dad and Mum were still able to do little things like meals and a bit of housework, they were not able to go out and about easily, so they took on the task temporarily, while Fred and Samantha were away that week.

So that taken care of, they could now decide where they would go. Each had their preferences, so it was a case of putting down names on paper and seeing if they could find one place where they would go. It finally came down to the South Coast of Devon, so that eventually was agreed. They also decided to go Express Road Travel. It was now that they should book the tickets for overnight travel, leaving, they found out, at 8pm on Sunday evening, from the village pick-up point.

The five-star hotel was booked by the travel agent, and the hotel taxi service would be waiting at the dropping-off point, all arranged by the agent. So it would appear that all necessary arrangements had been made, and Jenny and the others were able to relax, temporarily.

The Davidsons of Sunny Brook Farm had already arrived and were living with Samantha. They had visited the Taylors before and were greeted with open arms, as is the custom, also saying what a fine young man Fred was. He had also been down to Kent and Sunny Brook Farm to visit on several occasions with Samantha, when the time on the farm would allow, usually with Joe and Doris looking after things for a day or two while he was away. Vera, Samantha's Mum, was keen to see that her daughter had everything that she wanted on her special day. She had also been involved with Jenny in some of the visits that had been made. Of course, Jenny was the main protagonist, because she was the one that everyone in the village knew, and was the one they were familiar with.

William, Samantha's father, was a farmer of mainly arable crops, so although he had a wide and varied knowledge of farming, animal welfare was not something that he had indulged in over the years. Talk about root crops, and he is in his element, but it's as he said, you learn something new every day. Will had said that if there was anything he could do to help, then just ask. Dress suits to be worn by the men, hired for the occasion from a local firm, flowers for the bride-to-be, and buttonhole flowers for the men: all these things were arranged by Vera and Jenny, with some flowers to go to the caterers for arrangements on the tables, page girls with floral head circles, etc.

The Davidsons' son, who was still at University, would not be able to attend his sister's wedding to Fred because at that moment he was in South America as part of his PhD course in Botany, which was something he had always wanted to do. He felt it would help him when some day he had to take over from his dad, Bill. Saturday was the day when a rehearsal was arranged by the vicar, so that the couple to be married knew what to do and say during the wedding. The best man, being Joe, was given the ring to put on Samantha's finger and Bill, Samantha's Dad, the ring for Fred, so the proceedings continued until the completion was done, so they were all familiar with the day's events.

The day of the wedding arrived, and Jenny went round the various locations to pick up the children, to take them to Samantha's house. That was at 11 am. The flowers and the girls' headdresses had arrived at the various destinations, at the banquet hall and Samantha's house as well as at Old Oak Farm, where they would assemble before going on to the Church. At 2 pm, Jenny was making sure that everything was going like clockwork: she checked that all the guests were there, and that the transport had arrived to take them on to the church. So far, so good. She got Fred to keep an eye on things, because she had to go to Samantha's house, being the Maid of Honour.

The time came to go, so Fred and Joe ushered all the guests onto the bus. They arrived at the Cchurch 15 minutes before the proceedings were due to start. Then that last 15 minutes, as Fred put it, seemed to him to be an eternity, but it did arrive and Samantha on her dad's arm walked elegantly down towards the altar, and towards the man she loved. Fred was afraid to look, but he had to, she was so beautiful. The feeling welled up inside him – he later said it was hard to bear – then the ceremony took place. The vicar said, "I now pronounce you man and wife; Fred, you may kiss the bride."

The parents and best man and maid of honour went into an anteroom to sign the register, and the wedding vows were taken and the proceedings done.

The guests were invited to the Village Hall to partake in a banquet of food and wine. They arrived to find that their named places were set, and after the speeches, the food would arrive, and there would be music from the usual Saturday night quartet, who would play some popular music and some old-time tunes, for the older generation. When this was announced, the old folks gave a cheer. Bill (William), Samantha's dad, gave a rousing speech, with one or two jokes, and praising Fred his new son-in-law, and that he now had someone to call on if he needed help. Joe made a speech about the future prospects.

The proceedings went down particularly well: from the speech made by Joe, it seemed that there was quite a lot of hidden possibilities implied in just a few words. Now it was time for Samantha and Fred to beg leave of the assembly, to go and change to travel on their honeymoon down to Devon.

The guests went on partying until the small hours. Refreshments, beer, wines and spirits were provided by the caterers, so no one need go elsewhere, it was all there. Payment had to be made at the bar when requiring drinks.

Joe decided that maybe this was a good time to have a word with Desmond about his well-thought-out idea of an adventure into foreign climes: his thoughts of going to South America, to Argentina, to purchase a farming business there, to follow the trail of those Welsh people, who in 1865 settled a Welsh colony in Patagonia. A Preacher, a Michael D Jones, took some settlers on the ship Mimosa from Liverpool. They comprised 56 married adults, 12 single women, 33 single or widowed men and 52 children. They settled near the Chubut river, which later became known as Rawson. Joe found out that farming in Patagonia was a lucrative business and thought that together they could set up a good company out there and become very prosperous.

He called Desmond and Sue to one side and he and Doris went through the whole saga of what they had established, that there were farms being sold frequently and the owners retiring to big cities and spending the fruits of their labour, over the years, on luxury living, and that prices were comparatively cheap in comparison with New Zealand and the UK. Desmond and Sue said they would need to have a think about it, but on the face of it, it seemed to be a good idea.

Joe said, "We need to do some more research."

They thought Doris's Dad would buy Joe's farm. That would put him back to where he was before selling to the local council, so that was a possibility.

Desmond said, "I don't think we would have any difficulty selling our farm. There always seems to be people making enquiries about farms coming up for sale in our area," so they decided that they would look into it and be in touch as soon as they got home. They left it at that.

But you know Jenny, ears pricked, wanted to know what was going on, so Doris told her that she would tell her later.

A few days went by and Jenny, at every opportunity, was nagging at Doris to tell her what was going on after the wedding. She said, "You were all huddled together, you were obviously up to no good."

Doris said, "Not true, not for little nosy girls."

Jenny, red-faced, said, "Well, if you've got nothing to hide, then why won't you tell me what's going on?"

"OK, you are a persistent little devil," Doris said. Then she went on to tell Jenny about what they might do, and all about it. She also told Jenny not to say anything to anyone else.

During the following week, Joe and Doris had a word with Doris's dad and asked him if they went through with the plan that they would move, they didn't tell him where, would he buy Joe's farm? Joe's mum had no further use for the farm and had handed the deeds over to Joe. Would Jim be interested in buying it? Well, Jim was rather taken aback by this, and asked why they would want to move. Joe told him that there was nothing definite at the moment, but he would be the first to know if the plan went forward. Jim told him that he would be interested, but since Fred was doing all the work these days, it was only right that he should have a say in the matter, so the answer was yes, provisionally.

Doris, at the first opportunity, had a word with Fred and told him that she and Joe had spoken to Dad, who would first speak to him. Fred told her that it would be OK by him, but why did they want to move? She told Fred it had been on their minds for some time, but it was not yet final, and she would tell him more later.

The next thing to do was to inform Desmond and Sue that Doris's dad had offered to purchase Joe's farm, and that they only wanted Desmond and Sue to complete their sale so that the plan could be implemented. The whole episode had to be arranged on the basis that when the purchase of the New Farm in Rawson, Argentina, the transactions taking place in the UK as well as in New Zealand could all be implemented at the same time. A well-known group of international solicitors took on the task, with their counterparts in New Zealand and Argentina in close co-operation agreeing that they could take on the transition. The news soon came that Desmond and Sue had a suitable buyer for the farm and were quite prepared to wait until all the transactions had been completed.

There were three farms on the market near Rawson, so the thing to do was to go to Argentina, to choose a property and land that suited their needs. They had to go to the Argentinian Embassy in the UK and New Zealand to arrange for visas to travel: until they had made the final arrangements to go permanently, there was no point in securing residency papers, so for the time being a visa was all that was required.

Doris informed Sue that she would book a hotel in Rawson for the four of them. Desmond had relatives in New Zealand who would look after the children while they were away, so arrangements were made between Doris and Sue that they would meet in Buenos Aires International Airport, then a local flight would take them down to Rawson.

The 850-mile journey from Buenos Aires would take approximately three hours in air time, but it was better to meet there before the final trip, so that they could refresh themselves about things that hade transpired since their last get-together in the UK. Although they could have phone calls and contact by letter and other means, it was not quite like having a face-to-face talk. It was agreed that that was what they would do.

Joe had arranged with Fred to look after the farm while they were away. It would no doubt give Fred an insight into what would transpire, if eventually the farm was sold to Fred's dad and he had to look after it.

The time had to be set that, coming from different directions and time zones, the time to arrive at Buenos Aires had to be fixed, so that was a conundrum that had to be worked out. It was suggested that the arrival time had to be in the early morning, so that it gave a lot of daylight hours to become acquainted with the area, before setting off on their visits to the farms up for sale.

All was finally agreed and the plane flights booked. Everything was finally organised, and representatives of the international solicitors were informed of the proceedings, so that if they wished, one of their reps could attend the meetings.

Jenny could see what was going on, and from time to time badgered Doris into giving her more information. She asked Doris if it would be OK to mention this to Carlton, now that things were in the final stages. Doris told her, "Well if you must you must," knowing that before long, he would be part of the family anyway.

Jenny had made a date to see Carlton that evening, and as always, when Jenny had her mind set on something, she had to get it off her chest, so Carlton was going to have to listen to what Jenny had on her mind. She had been mulling it over for some time, since she first heard of the plan to emigrate to Rawson. She put the question to Carlton: was he interested? Did he think, as she did, that it would be a good adventure, to start a new beginning in a foreign land?

Carlton was not so sure about having to start from scratch again, since he had had quite a bit of help to get where he was at the moment. But once Jenny had her mind set on something, it took an awful lot to get her to change it. Carlton did try, but to no avail; she was steadfast, and in fact, as the evening progressed, and with more than a little persuasion and persistence, Carlton began to waver, until in the end he gave in, and asked Jenny what he might do to help.

Jenny had asked Doris whether while she was out there she would make a few enquiries about vacancies for school teachers. English was a subject that Jenny could teach well. Also, having taken a course in Spanish in high school would be advantageous in Rawson. She also asked Doris to find out about police positions for detectives for Carlton, who had also taken a Spanish language course in high school. Jenny told Carlton there was little they could do at the moment until final preparations were underway, so he should just sit tight for now, which is what they did, although Jenny was itching to get on with it. The rest of the evening went on as planned.

Doris and Sue had already agreed that a good time to visit would be in November, after the lambing season was over in the Southern Hemisphere. Then they could see how things had gone, how many new lambs had been born and so on. From the milk herd point of view, there would be little change.

Joe also had it in mind that beef for the American market was a consideration: as was previously mentioned, this was part of the package. It was now mid-October and only a few weeks away from the 8th of November when they had to meet at Buenos Aires at 6 am local time, so overnight trips from both locations were the order of the day.

The 8th of November arrived, and Joe and Doris said goodbye to their friends and relatives and were on their way to Argentina. They were dressed in normal winter clothing, because the average temperature in Rawson would be around 14 degrees C, and would gradually rise during their stay. Likewise, Desmond and Sue had set off on their journey to Buenos Aires, where they would meet to continue their journey to their destination at Rawson.

The journey overnight was uneventful. Joe and Doris had to wait for the aircraft from New Zealand to arrive, and when it did they all met, and there were hugs and kisses all round, they were so pleased to see each other. They had to wait for an hour for the connection to arrive to take them to Rawson, which gave them ample time to discuss their intentions when they arrived there. The plane eventually arrived, they boarded and were on their way to their destination. Three hours later they were in Rawson. They were met by a courier who took them to their hotel. He was the representative of the international solicitors who would co-ordinate the final agreement.

The meal they had been waiting for was now available in the dining room. They were shown to their rooms, had a quick wash and change and met each other at the table provided for them. The courier provided them with a list of the times and locations they had suggested, which should be adhered to as closely as possible. They looked over the arrangements and agreed that it was OK, and that would suit them fine.

Joe noticed a picture of the irrigation system that had been in operation in the late 18th and early 19th centuries, which the Welsh settlers had to construct to survive in the early years. Apparently, there was some talk of giving up the settlement and returning to the UK, but the Rev Jones persuaded them to carry on. The land was more like a desert in the early days, then history records that it was Rachel Jenkins who had the idea that, because the river Camwy on occasions burst its banks and brought life to the arid land that bordered it, a simple method of irrigation could be required to make the land fertile. So an irrigation system was installed, and the land began to flourish.

The migrants then became more settled, and today Rawson is a vibrant town. Joe knew of the history of the settlement, hence the reason for his enthusiasm. There was still some pampas land towards the Andean mountains where sheep did graze. Joe suggested to Desmond that that might be a factor to bear in mind during their visits to the farms. Desmond, on the other hand, was used to farming sheep on the flatlands, which of course Joe knew all about.

The next day was the day when the courier-guide was to take them to visit the three farms they were here to see. It was an early start, but that was not unusual for farmers, up at the crack of dawn. They wanted to see the farms that were near to the river but extended into the foothills of the Andes mountains.

Trelew was first on the agenda. The hacienda was beautifully constructed, an eight-bedroomed building with lots of outhouse constructions to house cattle and sheep. The main stock was Cheviot, 487 in all, with a few Jacob and Corriedale sheep, for personal reasons. The farm was managed by a pleasant fellow, of local Indian origin, who spoke fluent English and Welsh, as well as his native Spanish. They toured the farm, knowing what they were looking for, checking stock, and generally assessing the value that they were prepared to pay.

Trelew was the nearest farm to the town of Rawson, so that had to be considered. A price was given for the total allotment, and they agreed to consider it and let them, the owners, know in a few days. But before they left they thanked the manager for his courtesy, said goodbye and were on their way to Gaiman, which was a few miles further on along the river.

A very similar situation was found at Gaiman: beautiful layout, lots of living space, plenty of outhouses for the stock, also managed as before, nice man, well-mannered, who was very helpful in showing them round the farm. The main difference was that the sheep were Romney, 524 of them, with 73 Suffolk, favoured by the owner. They had a good look round, came up with a price they were prepared to pay, did a more thorough look around the accommodation, made a few notes, then had a general talk with the courier, who incidentally was a surveyor, to get his thoughts on the establishment, then decided to leave. They thanked the Manager and said goodbye before embarking on a longer journey towards the final destination, which was towards the foothills of the Andean mountain range.

They were glad of the rest. The third farm took five hours to reach by road, but some of the scenery was beautiful and when they did arrive, they were greeted by the owner of the farm. He wanted to show them round himself and was very knowledgeable about farming generally. Refreshments were offered and thankfully accepted. His English was good – he had been educated in the UK – while his Welsh was good because of his association with this Welsh-speaking community. He didn't want to move to the big city but was quite content to spend the rest of his days here in Trevelin. But he wanted to retire, he was saying he had a beautiful house nearer to the town, and would retire with his wife and live there. His sheep flock, he was saying, consisted of Suffolk 728, and another 305 Romney, and some 204 Speckled Face lambs, out on the hills. He also had 42 Alpaca which he grazed. The hacienda consisted of two separate buildings with enough outhouses to accommodate 2,500 animals. He also grazed a beef herd of 345 Herefords, which was quite a handful.

Joe and Desmond looked at each other with a knowing smile, and nodded. That was the signal that they could cope. The owner told them the price he was asking for the farm. Joe and Desmond told him that they liked what they had seen, but could he lower the price a little? After some thought, he gave them a reduced price. They told him they would have to give it some thought, but would let him know before they left.

They decided to stay another two days and book a hotel in Trevelin, to have a look around the area. They told the courier their intentions and arranged with him to settle the bill at the hotel in Rawson. The courier took them to a hotel he knew. They booked in and stayed over. They hired a car, which they could hand back in Rawson, after spending two days in Trevelin.

While there, they visited the Nant and Fall falls, a spectacular view, also the Flower Mill area, first established in the 1860s by the first settlers. The area was to their liking and they thought this was a great place to establish their roots: the most beautiful views, and the snow-covered mountain range was spectacular. It was obvious from their attitude that they had made their choice. This was the place where they wished to live. Everything was as near-perfect as they thought they could attain. They had promised to meet their courier in Rawson on their return from Trevelin. They were to meet at the hotel they had left three days earlier. He would then convey to the owner of the farm they visited in Trevelin the necessary documents to purchase the farm.

Before they left Trevelin, they visited the farm and saw the owner and told him their intent to buy, and that the documentation would be forwarded to complete the transaction by the international solicitors appointed to carry out the legal documentary requirements. Now that they had arrived back at Rawson, they had to arrange their return journey to their destinations, New Zealand and the

UK. They would fly back to Buenos Aires together and then depart back to their temporary homes, before they finally left to live permanently together in Trevelin, Argentina. They realised that, because of the distance between Rawson and Trevelin, any meetings that may have to take place should be held in Trevelin rather than Rawson, so a local flight from Buenos Aires to Trevelin Airport would be better.

The time arrived for them to leave, they said goodbye to Alyn, the courier, thanked him for what he had done, and hoped to see him in the not-too-distant future. They boarded the flight to Buenos Aires and were quite pleased with what they had achieved. Now that they had committed themselves, they were talking about how they would manage the stock they had just bought. All of them had an input as to how things should be managed. The discussion went on for some time, until a final agreement was reached. They left it at that and said final arrangements could be made onsite. By this time they had arrived at the airport.

The most important thing they had decided was that before they departed for their rehabilitation in Argentina, Sue and Desmond should sell their farm and come over to Joe and Doris at their farm to live, where they would have time to decide plans for the future, then they could all depart together to 'The Promised Land', as Joe called it. They hugged and kissed each other before they left, each going their separate ways, for the time being, to the UK and New Zealand.

When Joe and Doris arrived, the first thing they did was to go to the Care Home to see Joe's mother. She was fine, as well as could be expected. Doris's Mum and Pop visited her regularly, and she was having the very best attention that could be provided. They then went to Old Oak Farm to see Doris's mum and dad. The next two hours were spent explaining what they had seen, how beautiful the scenic view of the mountain range was, what they had decided to do, the size and look of the farm, and the two haciendas that would house both families. They were so excited with the prospect. Jim asked Gladys if, when Joe and Doris went to live there, should they go and visit? They seemed almost as excited as Joe and Doris. Then Fred and Samantha came into the room. They had been working, so the story had to be started all over again. Fred looked at Samantha, saying, "We must visit."

They had informed Tom and Fiona of their intensions, and since they were committed to attain their own ambitions, they wished them lots of luck and hoped they would succeed in their endeavours. They left Oak Farm and went back to their farm Tree Tops, after thanking Fred and Samantha for looking after things while they were away. Their intention was to settle down and prepare for the coming few days, where as well as looking after the farm, they had to prepare to meet the solicitors, along with Doris's dad to arrange the transfer of deeds from Joseph Martin to James Taylor. It so happened that the solicitors were one and the same for both parties: this made the transfer much easier, than if they were different.

They settled down to have a rest, when who should arrive to visit but Jenny and Carlton. The saga had to be gone through once more, but this time it was more like an interrogation. Both Jenny and Carlton wanted to know all about the place. What they had found out about teachers' requirements and vacancies? What was the police service like? Would they both be able to get employment? Doris told them that if they came with them, they could help out on the farm until they could find suitable jobs. This seemed to allay any fears they may have had. Jenny and

Carlton looked at each other and nodded their approval. The rest of the evening was spent talking about what they might do when they get there, and Doris and Joe's perception of the town of Trevelin.

The next two days were hectic, in that the conveyancing of the transfer of Joe's farm to James Taylor was completed. Fred, Jim Taylor's son, had now both farms to attend to, which Fred relished the thought of. At least now the Old Oak Farm was getting back to its size in former days and could live up to its former glory. Joe and Doris occupied the farm premises until their departure abroad, then Fred and Samantha would move in as their permanent residence. They could if they wished move into Jenny's cottage, but that would probably be rented out as before.

Joe and Doris had been notified by the international solicitors that Sue and Desmond's property and land had been sold and the conveyancing completed. The goods they wished to take to Argentina had been packaged and sent on by cargo boat to their destination. Joe and Doris had also completed the same task. The next message was that Desmond, Sue and the children were about to embark on their flight to the UK, giving them the time of their arrival at the airport. Before they arrived, Joe and Doris were in the airport arrival lounge. The greeting was as is usual: lots of hugs and kisses. The children were enjoying the experience. Of course, they were much older now and could understand more of what was going on.

They departed the airport and proceeded to their destination at Joe's and Doris's former residence, where they would stay for a week or so before their departure to Trevelin. They settled in after first visiting Joe's mum and then going on to Old Oak Farm, to see Doris's mum and dad. Fred and Samantha were there also to greet them, then they went on to their temporary home now at Tree Tops Farm. They didn't have time to settle down before Jenny and Carlton came in, beaming. Carlton came with the news that his dad had been in touch with the Chief Constable of Trevelin and had arranged for Carlton to take a crash course in Spanish (although he had been taught it when in high school), and having completed that, he would be offered a post as assistant to the Prison Governor. He was thrilled at the prospect. Jenny was also keen but mainly because Carlton was settled in a job, which he thought would be good experience to finally, in later years, becoming Governor.

So they were going too. Jim and Gladys were not pleased that some of the family were leaving them but implied that if that was what they wanted to do, although it was too much to ask for them to visit them, because they were their twilight years, they could come back to visit as and when they chose to.

Joe and Doris had been in touch with Tom and Fiona to let them know the situation, and they had promised that as soon as the families had settled into their new accommodation, they would visit.

Jenny and Carlton had to hand in their resignations to the various bodies which they served. That done, they were now ready to go to, as Joe put it, the Promised Land. Suitcases packed, everything that was required on the flight, all the items the children may need ready, so it was now getting time for them to depart. The tears flowed, the sobbing increased as they said goodbye to Joe's mum, Doris's and Jenny's mum and dad and to Fred and Samantha. It was a long farewell as they went into the departure lounge ready for take-off. They boarded the plane and as they said goodbye to the land they had known and loved for so long, the children asked why everyone was crying and were told that they may never see it again, that it was precious because it was the place they had known for so long. Peter told Sue she cried when they left New Zealand and was told that it was because it held so many memories of days gone by.

The children had become excited at the thought of their new home and a new beginning for them all. The flight was uneventful, and they arrived in Buenos Aires, collected their luggage and proceeded to the departure lounge of the next flight which would take them down to their final destination at Trevelin. They had time to take on refreshments and drinks before their departure.

They Arrived at Trevelin three hours later that morning and entered the departure area to find Alyn the currier waiting to meet them. To their surprise, the previous owner of the farm was there too. He had been notified of their time of arrival and wanted to meet them. They got into the transport provided and made their way to the farm. The previous owner was familiar with the running of the farm, even though he had three gauchos looking after the stock for him, and of course, he wanted to see them established in the haciendas and wished to see them settled and able to carry on the good work that had been his livelihood for more than 30 years. He told them before he left that if there was anything they wanted, or were not sure about, to get in touch with him and he would assist in any way he could. They thanked him for his kindness and said they would take up his offer should the need arise. Before he left, he introduced the three gauchos to their new bosses. They could speak a little English. Alyn was there as an interpreter so he could convey any part of the conversation they couldn't understand.

Joe and the family could all speak school Spanish, so it just needed them to brush up on the language, so that they could be more fluent in future.

They looked round the rooms, which were bare. The furniture had not arrived as yet, so it was a case of making do with what little they had. They had to quickly do a shop in the town, to find the things that were an urgent necessity. A refrigerator with food had been left by the owner, and a few cups, a kettle and a towel, so there was no urgency for food or drinks at the moment. The priority for Doris and Sue was to organise the eating arrangements, to get the food and anything they thought would make life a little easier at the moment. They decided to all bunk up in one building for the time being; separation and re-organising could be done after the furniture arrived. Things were not as cosy as they would have liked, but as Joe was saying, "The people who settled there from Wales, how would they have coped? But they did. At least we have a roof over our heads."

The weeks went by. The furniture arrived, and Joe and Desmond had been out on the farm looking and checking the stock with the gauchos. The result from them both was that everything was in good shape: the sheep and cattle were top quality, well looked after, so now the planning for the future could go ahead. The gauchos had been a great help while they were getting themselves established, but they were a costly addition to the farm budget, and they decided that one of them would have to leave. The younger one of the three, whose name was Vini, had no other commitments but himself, so it was decided he should be the one to go.

They had been in touch with the previous owner of the farm, just as a courtesy call, and while doing so, mentioned that their intention was that Vini's employment would be terminated. Manuel Romero, the previous owner, mentioned that Vini could come and work for him as a gardener, which was great, so they informed Vini that Senior Romero would employ him as a gardener. He was very pleased when they told him what had happened and thanked them ("Muchas gracias") for doing so.

Joe and Des had to go to the local abattoir, and to the local packing factory, so that when the sheep or cattle had to be culled, they could familiarise themselves with the procedure. On looking over the premises of both, they were not particularly happy with the hygiene and thought that they could improve on what they had seen. They realised that it would take time, but they had it in mind to have a new packing unit built, and adjacent to it an abattoir of their own. Alternatively, they could try to purchase what was available and improve on that, for the time being. They put the proposition to both parties, and to their surprise, the offer for both was accepted.

They employed the international solicitors to carry out the conveyancing for them. The reason they had so much cash left was because prices of land, etc., were so much cheaper. They employed an architect in the UK to create plans in Spanish, for the local planning office. Both premises would have complied with UK regulations, which was exactly what they wanted. The plans of the structures now in place had to be modified: these were sent to the UK for that to take place. A local builder would be employed to carry out the work. In the meantime, Joe and Des were busy contacting their American customers and others, to inform them that they would be able to supply meat already packed to UK standards in the next month. Local farmers, hearing of this, were quick to offer their produce to this consortium for culling and packing also. They had hardly had time to settle in when floods of orders were arriving to be commissioned. In less than a month, the buildings were modified, the current employees were retained, and because of a stricter hygiene control regime, more people had to be employed, for which the Mayor of Trevelin was very pleased.

Carlton had made an appointment to see the Mayor and the Police Chief. The course he had to attend had been arranged, and he had to attend the next day. The whole household were on a crash course in Spanish, as previously mentioned: a tutor had been commissioned for this purpose, so evenings were spent reading, writing, and speaking in Spanish. Even during the day they were all trying to converse in Spanish.

The days and weeks rolled by. The business was thriving; Des had made similar pens to house lame sheep, as he had done in New Zealand; Carlton had taken the post of Deputy Prison Governor; Jenny was employed by the education authority to teach English. She and Carlton had a civil wedding. It was a very joyous occasion. There was talk about going home to the UK to have the wedding with the folks back home, but everyone seemed so preoccupied for one reason or another, so that fell through. Jenny and Carlton lived in the same accommodation with Doris and Joe while Sue and Des had their own hacienda. The two children were attending the local school; in fact, at one stage, the children were teaching the grown-ups Spanish, which seemed a little odd.

Joe's mum's health was deteriorating rapidly, according to a message sent by Doris's mum and dad, so the decision was made that they should return home for a short time. Could Desmond cope? He intimated he could, with the help of the gauchos, so they booked flights and were quickly on their way. They arrived and went down to the nursing home where Gladys and Jim were waiting, knowing of their arrival. Joe's mum was not well, to say the least, but she perked up a little when Joe and Doris came in, she was so pleased to see them. Jim told them they should stay at Old Oak Farm, which they did.

They visited every day for a week, and Joe's mum asked who was looking after the farm in Argentina. She told them to go back and attend to business. They told her, "If you think we should, we will," so they hugged and kissed her and said goodbye.

When Joe came away he could not control his emotions. He cried and wept, tears rolling down his cheeks. Doris had a difficult job in trying to console him, but finally, he pulled himself together, and they made their way back to Old Oak Farm. Jim and Gladys were waiting; they told Joe they would visit his mum regularly and make sure she was comfortable.

Joe and Doris saw Fred and Samantha at the farm and had a good old chat about things. Doris pointed to Samantha and asked when was it due. "In three months' time," she told her. "Another Taylor on the way."

Before their departure, Doris and Joe promised that they would come and spend two weeks with them the next time they came. The other members of the families had mentioned that when it was convenient to return home, they would do so, as would Sue, whose family were in Perth, Australia, and Desmond's in New Zealand, they would also take the opportunity to visit their folks.

Doris had been helping out in the shop, which was now nearing its final stages: so little trade, just the things that other shops were not able to provide. Then it was goodbye once again, tears and hugs before leaving.

The news when they arrived back at Trevelin was that Joe's mum was not well, but still carrying on. Things on the farm were still progressing as usual. Des was glad to see Joe's return: the paperwork was beginning to pile up, and orders and enquiries were getting out of control. Sue and Jenny were trying to help. Carlton was so tied up with prison work, he just didn't have time to do anything else. Joe told them things would soon get sorted out, and he was right: within a day or so, things were sorted.

The next move was to register the company. Joe suggested that they should do that in the UK and the Company name should be, he told Des, 'The Martin Taylor Tromans Consortium'. Asked what he thought, Desmond told Joe he thought that was good, it had a certain ring to it, so that was adopted, and the girls also agreed. The international body were again informed and would carry out their instructions.

The plans for the upgraded abattoir were completed and the packing station modernised. Now things could go full speed ahead with orders they had received. One order Joe mentioned was from an American Company who had asked if the consortium could supply "1,000 12oz Steaks from the fifth rib," to which Joe had replied, "You bet." They were to be distributed, by them, to their five-star restaurant chain in the US. The packing station was inundated with orders for their produce to be packed and frozen ready for transportation.

The days and weeks rolled by. The business became a tremendous success, Joe and Des and Doris and Sue were extremely pleased with the outcome of their spirit of adventure, and it all came from Joe's experience at the university way back when he was studying agriculture at Aberystwyth in South Wales. The seed was sown: Joe had the wanderlust, first to New Zealand and now to Argentina. I think this may be his last move, unless of course, in his dotage, he may choose to come back to his roots in the UK.

The families, the Taylors and Martins, together with others they had collected on the way, were now, it appeared, established in the foothills near the Andean mountains, at Trevelin, where they established new roots, like those from Wales who came before them, in the middle of the 18th century: Welsh-speaking as a second language. Also English was spoken widely.

In later years as time went by, the families consisted of the following. Doris didn't have any children. Sue and Joe, while they were married, had two, Jill and Peter. Fred and Samantha had two boys and a girl; one of the boys, when he was older, went over to live with his Aunt Doris and Uncle Joe, in Trevelin. Tom and Samantha didn't have children: they chose a carrier in the RAF. Carlton and Jenny – who often talked of the good old days, when Jenny had the wink and when Maud got herself entangled with a married man, many moons ago now – they had three children. Like Fred and Samantha, one of their boys, having heard of the escapades and the Seven Sisters caves, now wanted to experience it for himself, so he came over to the UK and stayed with Aunt Samantha and Uncle Fred.

Fred and Samantha also visited the families in Trevelin and stayed with Doris and Joe. Of course, the lads were grown up and able to look after Old Oak Farm without their dad's help. But one thing that did happen for years, was that the families arranged every year to meet at Old Oak Farm, to celebrate Christmas. Joe's mum and Gladys and Jim had long since gone, but the memories and the roots of those that had gone before.

They remained as strong as ever, often talked about, the shop and the lime kilns, the headless chicken, how Joe had decided to emigrate to New Zealand and Doris wouldn't go with him, Jenny's fateful journey through the village on market day, persuading her dad to let her live on her own in the cottage near the village, the dances on Saturday nights and the way Tom used to flex his muscles in front of the girls, to try to gain their attention: all these things, a recalling memory brings, they talked of all these things and more. But now, a new chapter begins, for new beginnings that it brings, the roots remain and will always be the same.

Joe did take on a political role, when the business was making lots of money, and Managers were appointed to run everything, and he eventually became Mayor of Trevelin. Doris was busy in the town's 'Women's Guild', which she started. Desmond and Sue went sight-seeing all over the world, spending quite a lot of the time going back home. When they went back to the UK, Desmond had promised himself all those years ago, that he would go down the 'Seven Sisters' cave. He carried out that pledge while Gladys and Jim were alive, but he never regretted the move to Trevelin, like Joe and Doris and Jenny and Carlton. And what was more surprising was that Tom and Fiona later moved out there too. Old Oak Farm still carried on, though, with Fred and Samantha at the helm, and their children to carry on with the farm forever, as was their intention.

www.ingramcontent.com/pod-product-compliance
Lightning Source LLC
Chambersburg PA
CBHW071507030726
47593CB00003B/1188

CUISINE: Japanese
DRINKS: Full Bar
SERVING: Lunch & Dinner
PRICE RANGE: $$$$
NEIGHBORHOOD: Quintana Roo
An upscale Japanese robata grill eatery offering traditional Japanese cuisine with a modern influence. Favorites: Ora King Salmon and Spicy Yellowtail Sushi roll. Impressive cocktail selection.

THE WHITE BOX
GRAND OASIS PALM
Blvd. Kukulcan, 52 998 881 7000
https://oasishoteles.com/en/restaurants/the-white-box
CUISINE: Seafood/Steakhouse
DRINKS: Full Bar
SERVING: Dinner, Closed Mon & Tues.
PRICE RANGE: $$$$
NEIGHBORHOOD: Quintana Roo
Fine dining inspired by a group of renowned chefs. Haute cuisine in small dishes. Great tasting menu. Favorites: Blackened prawns and Sea Bass. Impressive wine list. Only seats 20 so reservations recommended.

Chapter 4
NIGHTLIFE

This is a party town. All those Spring Breakers didn't come down here to gaze lovesick at the moon. They came to party, to get drunk off tequila and to dance to loud music and to get laid.

Maybe you did, too!

In El Centro, prepare yourself for music that throbs incessantly, that's loud, that's insistent.

Like any good vacation destination, Cancun is just as fun at night as it is during the day. Most of the nightclubs are located in the entertainment district at the northeast tip of the Hotel Zone. Here you can party the night away in one mega-club, or bar hop to your heart's content.

The mega-bars have made Cancun famous for its nightlife. These monster party complexes hold thousands of people. They feature a variety of acts and eye-catching visuals as well as world-class DJs.

The shows are constantly changing from moment to moment. At one moment you may be watching a contortionist, which might be followed by a bikini contest and fog machines. Internationally known performers regularly make appearances at these clubs. It is not uncommon to find such acts as Shakira or the Black-eyed Peas performing.

Coco Bongo is the oldest and most well-known of the mega-clubs, but others have come to prominence in recent years such as Bulldog, The City, Dady Rocks, and Dady O. Each of these places does its best to outdo the others, and we recommend visiting them on different nights. For those who haven't the time or stamina to visit one club a night there are nightclub tours that let you experience several of the mega-bars in one crazy night.

Drinks run $7 to $11.

It is not uncommon for the places to stay open until the sun comes up.

Here are some important tips for a safe and enjoyable night out in Cancun:

* Give your waiter a good tip up front, so they take care of you all night.

* Pay as you go, or you may be in for a big surprise.

* Keep your hands on your drink, and don't take a drink from a stranger. This goes for everybody, women and men alike.

* If you've been drinking heavily, DO NOT go home alone or try to drive a car. One thing you don't want to deal with is the Mexican police and judicial systems, pathetically corrupt as they are. Also, DO NOT travel home alone. Have someone with you or

take public transport. Don't even get into a cab alone if you can help it. You might end up in a ditch.

* Don't leave your camera sitting around. Better yet, don't bring a camera at all.

THE CITY

Boulevard Kukulcán – KM 9.5, Zona Hotelera, Cancun, Mexico: 52-998-883-3333 ext. 138 www.thecitycancun.com Cover runs $40-$50 (includes bar) or $25 without. Through the sprawling 3-floor and 8,000 square feet of space this huge club occupies, it's easy to get a drink – they have about 10 bars. Impressive light shows, state-of-the-art sound system, DJs imported from around the world. Though the club doesn't get started till 10:30 at night (runs till about 5 a.m.), the complex itself opens in the morning, so you can spend the day herein a cabana at the beach, by the pool. Plenty of food and drink all day and night. Different rooms offer different atmospheres. VIP Rooms. Celeb hangout.

COCO BONGO

Blvd. Kukulcan Km 9.5 Plaza Forum, Cancun,
Mexico: 52-800-841-4636/ 52-998-883-5061
www.cocobongo.com/
Cover runs $50 during the week and $10 additional
on weekends (includes open bar).
Many different kinds of music (salsa, hip-hop,
Caribbean, techno and everything else) gets played
here in one of the hottest clubs in town. (Holds over
2,500, but you'll still encounter lines). Here at CoCo
Bongo, the whole place is a dance floor, from the top
of the tables to the top of the bars. Famous around the
world for its theme parties.

DADY'O

Boulevard Kukulcán – KM 9.5, Zona Hotelera,
Cancun, Mexico: 52-998-883-3333
www.dadyocancun.com/
Cover runs about $20-$30.
Most established of the Grupo Dady cluster of clubs.
Like all the big clubs here, always seeking to out-do
each other, this one has a superior light & sound
system. Always packed.

DADY ROCKS

Boulevard Kukulcán – KM 9.5, Cancun, Mexico: 52-
52-998-883-3333
www.dadyocancun.com/
Cover runs $20-$30.
Slightly different package in this spinoff of Dady'O:
here you can get pretty good Tex-Mex food, live
bands, but there's still a DJ and dancing. Dining

begins at 6 p.m. on the terrace, and inside they open at 8. They have 4 bars, 2 floors, outdoor terrace, the top sound & light system, contests like Wet T Shirt, different ladies' nights, a Sexy Legs Contest (winner gets US$1500).

FORUM BY THE SEA
Paseo Kukulcán km. 9.5 zona Hotelera Cancún: 52-998-883-4425
www.forumbythesea.com.mx
WEBSITE DOWN AT PRESSTIME
Oceanfront area has it all. Here you'll find all sorts of nightlife activities: from sports bars to dance clubs, from cheapie taco stands to some of the best dining spots in the area. Lots of shopping as well.

LOBBY LOUNGE
RITZ-CARLTON
Retorno del Rey 36 | Zona Hotelera, Quintana Roo: 52-998-888-0808

www.ritzcarlton.com
For a much more subdued ambience, you'll find a small, intimate club in the Lobby Lounge in the Ritz-Carlton. It opens at 5 for drinks and light snacking, but later, there's a dance floor with a DJ. Not the young, raucous crowds you get in the big clubs. (They also offer 70 tequilas at the bar and they'll set up tequila flights for you.)

Chapter 5
ATTRACTIONS

TOURS

Everybody in Cancún has got a brother who runs a tour and they can get you a good price. Some of them really are good opportunities and others are rip-offs. We suggest you don't take any of these offers at first, and look around for a bit to get a sense of what is out there and how much it *ought* to cost. Prices fluctuate depending on the season and what conventions might be in town, so ask around. And remember, everybody is your friend when you've got money to spend.

WATER SPORTS

XEL-HA

Carretera Chetumal-Cancun km 240, Quintana Roo: 52-998-883-3143
www.xelha.com
A few miles south of Cancún is Xel-ha, which has transformed itself into a fantasy land of excitement and discovery for those who love the water and all things that live in it.

Here, you can swim with the dolphins for about $100 to $150, depending on how long you want to be in the water with them.

There are dozens of activities such as snorkeling, cliff jumping, tubing, scuba and snuba diving.

('Snuba' diving is for people who aren't certified to scuba dive. You wear a mask attached to tubes that rise to an oxygen tank floating on the surface. The tubes run around 20 feet. Quite liberating.)

They even have a devise called "Sea Trek," a large plastic piece of head gear you put on that covers your whole upper body and rests on your shoulders. You have great underwater views with this device.

The grounds are huge and feature many kinds of environments such as nature trails, cenotes, a giant lagoon, and underwater caves.

EL REY

If you are in Cancún and haven't the time or inclination to commit to a day trip to the further, more well-known sites, but still want to see Mayan ruins, then El Rey is the place for you. You don't even have to leave the city. El Rey is located at kilometer 17 in the south Hotel Zone. The bus goes right by it, and any taxi driver will know where it is.

SEA TURTLES

One of the most memorable events you can experience in Cancún is the turtle season. Cancún is home to two of the world's seven species of sea turtle – the Loggerhead and the Green Turtle. The hospitality industry on the beach is an instrumental player in the conservancy and protection of these endangered species. The laying season begins in April. Incubation lasts about two months, and the last eggs of the season hatch in October. During this season the hotels keep bright lights off the beach at night so as not to disturb the turtles, and many hotels have staff dedicated to sea turtle protection. It is very common to see turtles coming ashore to lay their eggs late at night. This is reported to the local conservancy and the eggs are quickly moved to a protected area where they can incubate in peace. When the baby turtles hatch, guests of the hotels are invited to witness the event and aid in their return to the ocean. Children and adults alike are moved by this magical experience and go home with a new insight into the need to protect the environment and all species of life on Earth.

WHALE SHARKS

The Summer months of June through September are Whale Shark season. During this time the warm waters of the Gulf of Mexico and the Caribbean Sea meet, causing an upswelling of plankton-rich water, which is a feast to these gentle giants. Whale Sharks are the largest fish in the Earth's oceans, sometimes growing to over 40 feet long and weighing over 20 tons. But don't worry, these magnificent creatures are not a threat to humans; quite the opposite, actually. During the summer months, Whale Shark tours leave Cancún daily, filled with happy tourists excited by the chance to actually swim among these giant fish.

SWIMMING WITH DOLPHINS
There are a number of dolphinariums located in Cancún, including some of the major hotels. We ask that you consider, however, avoiding these attractions. Dolphins are a highly social and intelligent creatures. They are taken from their life in the wide ocean and forced to live out an isolated existence restricted to a small, often artificial, area for the amusement of throngs of tourists. We prefer to leave our cetacean friends free in the wild.

CENOTES
One interesting fact about the Yucatán Peninsula is that there are no rivers. For various geological and

tectonic reasons, all water flows underground. The limestone rock covering reservoirs of water in many places has collapsed, leaving open-air sinkholes called Cenotes. These cenotes are often hundreds of feet deep, with crystal-clear cool water. Swimming in these cenotes is an interesting and exciting alternative to a day at the beach. We highly recommend you take at least one day to experience this uniquely Yucatecan pastime.

RUINS

It would be a shame to visit the Yucatán and not see Mayan Ruins. There are hundreds of known Mayan ruins. We list here the ones most convenient to visitors to Cancún. Take bug spray and plenty of water. And you might want to take some bananas to feed the ubiquitous iguanas.

TULUM

You've probably seen the stunning iconic pictures of a Mayan pyramid rising on a cliff above a sandy beach and turquoise waters. That's Tulum, the only significant site that was built on the ocean. Spanish sailors in the early 16th century recorded sailing by and seeing a thriving, colorful Mayan city where we now find grey ruins. The views and ambiance is stunning – our favorite, really. Tulum is located an hour and a half south of Cancún, and there are daily tours from most of the cities in the Yucatán. The site itself is not very large – one can take in the whole place in about an hour – but it is the most photogenic. We recommend arriving early in the day or later in the afternoon, for it can get quite crowded at times.

From the parking center one can take the tram for a small fee or walk the quarter mile to the site entrance. There is access to the beaches, so feel free to make a whole day of exploring the ruins then playing in the surf. The souvenir shopping center that has grown up at the parking lot is rather an eye-sore, and the prices are not good, despite what your guide will tell you.

COBA

Coba is about an hour and a half southwest of Cancún. Despite the distance, there are some good reasons to go see this site. Coba is the least restored of all the popular sites, and this gives it a wonderful Indiana Jones feel. There are many buildings that are still covered by jungle. The main pyramid is one of the largest, and visitors can still climb it and look out across the Yucatán jungle. The grounds are quite extensive, so we recommend renting bicycles at the entrance, which adds another enjoyable dimension to your excursion. Watching the crocodiles being fed in the lakes is always a thrill. There are many quaint shops along the road to Coba selling interesting tchotchkes at reasonable prices.

CHICHEN ITZA

Chichen Itza is the most popular Mayan site on the Yucatán peninsula. The site is listed as one of the Seven New Wonders of the World. It is a good distance from Cancún, but dozens of tour buses a day make the 2 ½ hour trek. We recommend having a guide for this site. Being the most famous and developed site, it is also the most restrictive. Visitors are not allowed in the buildings or to climb the pyramids. The guides provide a rich narrative to spark one's imagination and form a bond with the site. Excellent bilingual guides can be hired for a reasonable price at the entrance. Many visitors appreciate the mathematical accuracy and astrological alignment of the buildings. If possible, we recommend visiting on either the Spring or Fall Equinox, where you can join the thousands of people who come to watch the Descent of the Serpent, a shadow cast at just the right angle to create the appearance of a snake descending the Temple of Kukulcan. After a sweaty day of wandering around

Chichen Itza, we recommend you cool off with a refreshing dip in Ik Kil cenote, a few kilometers away.

ECO ADVENTURE PARKS

Recent years has seen a sharp rise in public interest in ecotourism; and the Yucatán Peninsula, with so much to offer the out-doors-minded traveler, has seen a boom in Eco Adventure Parks. Located within an hour or so of the city, these parks offer a wide range of exciting amusements from zip lines to horse riding to floating along underground rivers. Transportation is best arranged through the parks, as directions can often be vague. We recommend checking with your hotel for tickets, as they often have them at much better prices than you will find at the gate. Here are a few of our favorites.

AKTUNCHEN NATURAL PARK

Located about an hour south of Cancún, Aktun Chen offers an exciting mix of activities for all ages. The caves at this site are magical and we recommend the tour. If above ground is your thing, go way above ground on their zip line and suspended bridges tour, which travels through the jungle canopy for over a kilometer. They also have a six-acre wildlife zoo with an emphasis on conservation. And don't miss the chance to go swimming and snorkeling in their crystal-clear cenotes.

HIDDEN WORLDS CENOTE PARK

Hidden Worlds has taken tree-top adventure to a whole new level. Besides the regular zip lines, they also have a sky cycle which visitors pedal on lines through the trees. They're big attraction, however, is a new roller coaster style zip line. Scuba diving is offered in the cenotes and there is also a zip line that drops into a cenote. Cave rappelling is an interesting adventure, and when you're tuckered out with all the physical exertion, take a relaxing ride in a jungle buggy.   This attraction is about an hour and a half south of the city.

RIO SECRETO

This is one of our favorites. Located in Playa del Carmen, about an hour south of Cancún, Rio Secreto is a stunning series of caves and cenotes which will leave you speechless. There are caverns filled with so many thousands of stalactites and stalagmites that you will think you are in some surreal alien cathedral. This is a tour not to be missed.

SELVATICA

This award-winning eco theme park is closer to Cancún than most of the others, about half an hour south. There is a wide array of zip lines, cenotes to swim in, and lots of different kinds of vehicles to bump around the jungle trails on.

XAMAN HA AVIARY

The Xaman Ha Aviary is the place to go to see the wonderful variety of bird species that populate the Yucatán Peninsula. Here you can see Snowy Egrets, Pink Flamingoes, Scarlet Macaws and Toucans, among many, many others. Located in Playa del Carmen, the aviary is much better priced that many of the other attractions in the area, and photographers are welcome to bring their equipment at no additional charge.

XCARET

Xcaret is one of the largest and oldest eco parks in the Mayan Riviera. The park features archeological sites, underground rivers, beaches, lagoons and pools, as well as educational and interactive exhibits such as aquariums and greenhouses. There are many local species of animal to interact with. In the evening shows featuring the native Mayan legends and customs bring to life the rich and vibrant history of the area.

SIAN KA'AN BIOSPHERE

The Sian Ka'an Biosphere is a leader in ecological conservation and education. Located near Tulum, the center is a model of green technology and sustainable development. A UNESCO World Heritage Site, Sian Ka'an's million acres is home to many species of rare flora and fauna and over twenty archeological sites. Those who love nature and the peace and serenity it offers will find it to their heart's content. We highly recommend renting a kayak.

crafts

Chapter 6
SHOPPING & SERVICES

SHOPPING IN CANCÚN

If you haven't already spent all your money on cenote tours and all-inclusive resorts, there is lots of shopping in Cancún as well. The Hotel Zone has several large and modern malls featuring both Mexican handicrafts and international brands. There are also the requisite chain restaurants and cinemas just as in the US. We suggest you also make the effort to get out of the Hotel Zone and go into downtown Cancún, where you can find the famous Mercado 28, as well as all the chains you know and love in the US.

PLAZA LA ISLA

Blvd. Kukulcán km 12.5, Z.H., 52-998-883-5025
www.laislacancun.com.mx

This is one of the newest and trendiest of the shopping centers in the hotel zone. On the Nichupte Lagoon, the center is built on a series of canals, with bridges connecting parts of the center, all reminiscent of Venice. There are many shops of different types, most of them pricey. Our favorite place to wander here is the souvenir emporium, where one can find some good deals. Plaza la Isla also features restaurants, a disco, and cinema.

FLAMINGO PLAZA

Boulevard Kukulkan Km 11.5, Zona Hotelera, 77500 Cancún, Quintana Roo, 52-998-883-2855
www.flamingo.com.mx
It seems that all tropical Latin-American cities have a Flamingo Plaza. Cancún's is a stylish building of marble housing designer and duty-free shops. There are also lots of Mexican arts and crafts available. Food-wise Flamingo Plaza offers many restaurants, including chains such as Margaritaville, The Outback, Pat O'Brien's and Planet Hollywood.

PLAZA CARACOL

Blvd Kukulcan Km 8.5, Z.H. 2-998-883-4760
www.plazacaracol.mx/
Plaza Caracol is the biggest mall in Cancún. It is also very modern. It is centrally located on the Hotel Zone just north of the Convention Center. There are many boutiques, including favorites such as Benetton, Gucci and Ralph Lauren. There are also some very interesting art galleries. Prices at Plaza Caracol are pretty good – certainly better that what you'd pay in the US.

PLAZA LAS AMERICAS

Av. Tulum 260, Downtown, Cancún, 52-998-887-3863
Located downtown, Cancún's version of a home-town mall has everything to make you feel at home. There are a nice assortment of local boutiques, arcades and fast-food outlets. It also features a JC Penney and a Sears.

MERCADO 28

Xel-ha Mz. 13 SM 28, 77501 Cancún, Quintana Roo, Mexico: 52-998-892-4303
www.facebook.com/Mercado28Cancun
Mercado Veintiocho. This is Cancún's most popular place to shop for souvenirs. You will enjoy wandering through the many stalls filled with bargains. Here you will find the same items offered in the Hotel Zone, but at much better prices. Haggling for a bargain is part of the fun here, so don't settle for the first price given.

INDEX

WANT 3 FREE THRILLERS?

Why, of course you do!

If you like these writers--
Vince Flynn, Brad Thor, Tom Clancy, James Patterson, David Baldacci, John Grisham, Brad Meltzer, Daniel Silva, Don DeLillo

If you like these TV series –
House of Cards, Scandal, West Wing, The Good Wife, Madam Secretary, Designated Survivor

You'll love the **unputdownable** series about Jack Houston St. Clair, with political intrigue, romance, suspense.

Besides writing travel books, I've written political thrillers for many years that have delighted hundreds of thousands of readers. I want to introduce you to my work!

Send me an email and I'll send you a link where you can

download the first 3 books in my bestselling series, absolutely FREE.

Mention **this book** when you email me.

andrewdelaplaine@mac.com